A all of us with it!"

She slipped behind Regdar to face the orcs coming up behind them. They looked crazy, their eyes glassed over with rage. Orcs weren't temperate beasts under any circumstances, and this unexpected event probably had them lashing out at anyone they could blame. As the orcs drew close, Lidda used her lightness to her advantage by springing from her place and landing on the bridge's handrail. Her blade sliced an orc across its face. The orc squealed in pain and tripped backward. It broke through a portion of the far handrail as it tumbled off the bridge, joining its fellow in the ice below. Another swung its axe at Lidda, but she dodged the weapon easily and jumped to behind the orcs this time. She heard wood breaking beneath her feet and barely pulled away before the deck gave way with a loud crack.

**From the creators of the
greatest roleplaying game ever
come tales of heroes, monsters, and magic!**

By T.H. Lain

T.H. Lain

PLAGUE OF ICE

Distributed in the United States by Holtzbrinck Publishing.
Distributed in Canada by Fenn Ltd.

Distributed to the hobby, toy, and comic trade in the United States and Canada
by regional distributors.

Distributed worldwide by Wizards of the Coast, Inc. and regional distributors.

Printed in the U.S.A.

Cover art by Sam Wood and Matthew Mitchell
First Printing: March 2003
Library of Congress Catalog Card Number:

9 8 7 6 5 4 3 2 1

US ISBN: 0-7869-2953-7
UK ISBN: 0-7869-2954-5
620-17882-001-EN

U.S., CANADA,	EUROPEAN HEADQUARTERS
ASIA, PACIFIC, & LATIN AMERICA	Wizards of the Coast, Belgium
Wizards of the Coast, Inc.	P.B. 2031
P.O. Box 707	2600 Berchem
Renton, WA 98057-0707	Belgium
+1-800-324-6496	+32-70-23-32-77

Visit our web site at **www.wizards.com**

Prologue . . . The nameless city, for such it was even when it was inhabited, stood for well over a thousand years in the depths of the Fell Forest. It was not called the Fell Forest or any other name then. The wizards and sorcerers of the city introduced the gnoll tribes to the forest, hoping that they would discourage uninvited guests. The ploy worked beyond their wildest dreams, as few people visited in the ages since.

A millenium later, The city's basalt towers still stood, perfect and undamaged through centuries of neglect, a silent testament to the skill of those wizards who raised them from the earth. The city's builders formed a cabal of mages who turned their back on the world to pursue their research in secret, and it was a great experiment. The emblems of Uncaring Boccob and Wee Jas, deities of magic, were etched into the sides of each tower, in hope that those gods might bless the endeavor and watch over the city. In fact, no such thing happened.

No one knew any of this in the walled frontier cities of Atupal and Klionne, places remarkably lacking in curiosity regarding any history, including their own. Centuries after the abandonment of the towers, the residents of the closest towns had no idea that they shared a common origin; indeed, they had no idea that the towers even existed. The wizards' city was erected in a deep valley within the forest, so that even the tallest of its towers were not visible to the outside world. Thus was their privacy ensured. The location was so secret that mention of it survived only in scattered, ancient tombs and nearly forgotten myths.

The story of the city's fall was inglorious. No plague, no war or disaster claimed its inhabitants but merely time and waning commitment. The city's original inhabitants were content to lock themselves away with their books and spells, but the same was not true of their children and grandchildren.

Despite fears that the city's secrets would be lost, eventually malcontents were allowed to leave the city if they promised never to speak of its existence. Some of these emigrants established themselves as the heroes and rulers of an age. All kept their promises and never spoke of their home.

Still, the magicians' efforts to protect the nameless city proved fruitless. The city was never betrayed, but its vitality and life slowly ebbed away as later generations were drawn into the wider world. The experiment failed. As the last inhabitants grew old and died, the city was left to the ravages of the Fell Forest. Nature moved in, but even it could not erase the enchanted architecture. The towers remained. More importantly, locked away in the bowels of the city were potent artifacts of the wizards, items whose existence couldn't be hidden forever. Eventually, adventurers, antiquarians, and treasure-seekers came to the Fell Forest in search of power and knowledge.

Some stumbled upon the last remaining references to the nameless city and went looking for it. Others set out blindly across the Berron Bridge into the Fell Forest with little idea of what awaited them. Most would be killed by the orcs, gnolls, or other local menaces for their weapons and armor.

All of these seekers passed through Atupal or Klionne before jumping off into the forest, and they were unfailingly surprised by the locals' lack of interest in what might lie beyond the screen of trees. Some adventurers elected to pass through in secret to avoid drawing derision from merchants and farmers.

Such was the case with a group of four heavily armed humans who passed through Klionne. They made no mention of seeking the nameless city. Once inside the Fell Forest, all their skill was needed to evade wolf packs and fight off orcs. They found it nearly impossible to navigate through the dense timber. Tired and desperate, they eventually stumbled upon the legendary lost city, through luck as much as planning. The gnolls and orcs would not pursue them into its silent streets, and the adventurers foolishly assumed they were safe within its boundaries.

But the arcane architects were not fools, and their treasures were not for the unwary. The world might never know what triggered the eruption, but soon after the intruders' arrival, a torrent of cold poured from the city's central courtyard. The initial blast of frost was too much for the weakened humans, and it was only the first wave of an arctic deluge that would flow across the hills and valleys, destroy the Fell Forest, and ultimately threaten to bury the whole region beneath a glittering glaze of dazzling, deathly white.

I

"**You see those** snow-capped mountains over there?" Regdar asked.

"I sure do," answered Lidda. "What of it?"

"A week ago they weren't snow-capped."

"Oh." The halfling shielded her eyes and studied the distant range with new interest.

Pelor's sun shone warm overhead, but Regdar and Lidda were dressed in winter furs as they advanced through a grassy field a day's march outside of Klionne. Birds sang merrily and rabbits played nearby, blissfully unaware of the coming storm. Clouds gathered in the distance, sprawling their white-gray menace across the horizon.

"How much farther do you think it is?" asked Lidda. "I'm starting to sweat. That can't be a good thing. I could freeze when the temperature drops."

Regdar peered into the distance. "The scouts in Klionne said it's moving pretty fast. It won't be long now."

"I don't enjoy the cold, you know that?" Lidda said. "I can't imagine why I agreed to this mission."

"I can." Regdar cast her a half-smile. "It was the reward offered by the magistrate of Klionne. You should thank me for arguing on your behalf. He was wary of hiring a thief."

"A thief?" Lidda feigned shock. "Really, Regdar, you surprise me. Labels like that are so unfortunate. I expected better from you."

"Perhaps you've forgotten our first meeting."

Lidda stamped her foot restlessly. "How often are you going to drag that up?"

"As often as possible," Regdar said, "because the lies you tell about it get more amusing each time."

This was a game they'd played many times, and Lidda usually enjoyed it, but between the warm furs and the boredom of waiting, she was in no mood for it today. She let the dialog drop.

Minutes later, Regdar craned his neck upward. "I think I see something," said the warrior. He pointed into the distance. "Do you see it?"

By squinting, Lidda could barely make out a field of pale, frosted whiteness rising twenty or thirty feet off the ground like a roiling wall. As she watched, it grew noticeably in height. Whatever it was, it was headed toward them at an impressive speed.

Regdar faced this strange phenomenon head-on. It raced silently across the fields, generating no wind or vibration as it came, almost as if it wasn't there at all but was a massive illusion. As it drew near, it became clear that it resembled a wave, twisting and flowing as it raced forward, shimmering with shades of white and blue.

At points along its undulating surface, Lidda could see through the wall of white. The world was brighter on the other side, lit by the sun's dazzling reflection off the ground. Through the field's tint, a thick, blue layer of ice seemed to cover the earth. Lidda and Regdar felt like swimmers in the path of a tidal wave. Instinctively, Lidda closed her eyes and crouched as the wave passed over. She expected pain, but all she felt was cold.

The temperature dropped sharply, and even though the sun was still in the sky above them, its rays were weak, lending little of its heat to this new world. The contours of the land were the same, but it was covered with snow. Their feet were planted in it, and snow clung to their shoulders. Metal armor and weapons were instantly frosted.

Regdar and Lidda stood in the very same spot, except that where it had been summer, it was now winter.

"So it's like they said," Lidda observed, shivering lightly and shaking the snow from her hair. She'd half expected the tales to turn out to be a merry prank or the ravings of a drunken hermit.

Regdar nodded, his jaw clenched in muted tension. "Let's hurry. We should try to cross the River Berron by sundown. We're supposed to meet the party from Atupal there."

The neighboring cities of Atupal and Klionne had a lengthy history of friendly rivalry. At this moment it was a little less than friendly, owing to a trade dispute. Walled frontier cities familiar with orc raids and other dangers, they were generally insular places, content to keep to themselves and heavily distrustful of adventurers, but this strange, new development, this wave of winter fanning out from the little-visited Fell Forest, threatened both cities equally, so arrangements were made for Regdar and Lidda to meet a team dispatched from Atupal for the same purpose—investigation. The magistrate of Klionne privately issued dire warnings to them about not trusting this group too much. It was possible, he cautioned, that Atupal might even be behind the entire problem. Lidda doubted that and paid little attention to the magistrate's paranoia. In all likelihood, the people they would meet would not be Atupalans at all but convenient adventurers recruited to act on the city's behalf, just like Regdar and Lidda.

The two trudged through the snow, awed by this bizarre, new landscape. Under any other circumstances they would think it beautiful, like an untouched fairyland of brilliant white. The air was not oppressively cold but crisp and energizing, with only the barest wind, like a pleasant winter day. There are two kinds of cold, Lidda thought. One is this, a cold fit for making snowmen and snow forts and snowball fights, a cold that brings about rosy cheeks and warm mittens, the cold of fondly recalled childhood. Then there was vicious cold, the cold of frostbite and lost toes, of death, of frozen layers in the Abyss where foul gods ruled over ice-shrouded courts. Lidda knew this cold, too. It haunted the corners of her childhood, and she feared that she would know it again all too soon.

It was difficult to enjoy the snow even now. Knowing the strange and unnatural character of this cold zone made it hard for Regdar and Lidda to see it as anything other than a blot on the land and a potential threat to untold human lives.

It was much brighter now because of the sun reflecting off the carpet of untouched snow. The two of them needed to avert their eyes periodically, lest they be blinded. Turning to look behind them, Lidda saw their footprints trailing off into the distance and vanishing. Under other circumstances, she thought, this might make her laugh, but not today.

They continued on their way silently for most of the afternoon. Lidda thought seriously before putting her concerns into words.

"I've heard it claimed," she said, "that all the world, or at least a lot of it, was once frozen. The sages call it an 'ice age'."

"In my experience," said Regdar, "the sages frequently say things that can't be proven. It makes them seem smarter."

"Yes, yes, " Lidda said, "but what if this was true? What

made this ice age? What made it go away? What made the ice retreat to the far north only? Could we be seeing the beginning of a new ice age here?"

"Look, here's the river."

Regdar pointed out the bank of the River Berron, neatly changing the subject from the dire predictions Lidda was making. Neither of them had seen the River Berron before. In the blanket of white, the river was almost perfectly camouflaged from any distance away. As they stood overlooking it, they wondered what it looked like under normal conditions. It was reasonably wide, at least by local standards, but did it trickle or rush? Was it warm or cool? Did fish jump out of the water, and were those fish now frozen solid beneath the ice, waiting for a spring thaw that might never come? Regdar picked up a heavy rock and tossed it onto the frozen surface. It bounced.

Regdar checked the map given them by the magistrate of Klionne. It showed Atupal, Klionne and some lesser hamlets on the south side of the river and winding north of them the mighty Berron, crossed only by the Berron Bridge somewhat west of their current location. Detail of the far side was sketchy, as few except some dedicated hunters and adventurers crossed it regularly. The hunters didn't need maps, and the adventurers either didn't come back or didn't want anyone to know where they'd been. No logger ever touched the Fell Forest. Local lore suggested it was haunted by things far worse than gnolls. Beyond the forest stood the suddenly snow-capped mountains called either the Mountains of Klionne or the Atupalan Range, depending on where you lived. It was a small blessing, perhaps, that there were no inhabited centers on the other side of the river and under immediate threat.

"We should follow the river to the west," Regdar said. "It shouldn't be far to the bridge. From what the magistrate said, tribes of orcs and gnolls have been known to cross the bridge from time to time. We should be on the ready."

"Right," said Lidda, drawing her short sword from under her furs. Some time had passed since they last saw action, and she knew well that Regdar perked up noticeably after a good fight. She supposed combat was just another thing to get his mind off Naull. Lidda's blade glinted with frost. She wet her finger, ran it along the blade, and felt it stick to the metal.

The sun was almost sinking by the time they reached Berron Bridge, spanning a narrow section of river. It was obviously untended and in a fairly advanced state of decay. Nobody in his right mind would take a wagon across it, but they judged that two people could get across without any trouble. In a nearby tree, gnarled and dead, two songbirds confusedly chirped their winter calls. Some white mounds stood nearby, which they took as boulders placed near the bridge to mark out roads coming from different directions. Regdar knocked away the snow covering a sign next to the bridge. It said "Cross at Own Risk," though this should have been obvious to anyone but the blind. The only safety precaution was a rusty, metal handrail on either side of the bridge.

"I take it we're first," Lidda observed, scanning the area and seeing no sign of the other party. "Our friends from Atupal haven't arrived yet."

"Maybe they're not coming," said Regdar. "Maybe Atupal's withdrawn its services. Maybe they've gone ahead. But it's nearly dark. Let's cross the bridge and set up camp. We can wait for them there."

The two stepped onto the bridge, feeling with their toes for the uneven, wooden slats beneath the snow. The bridge creaked audibly under their weight.

"Take it nice and steady," Regdar advised.

"And don't look down," Lidda added, griping one of the

handrails, but she didn't take her own advice. The frozen river was twenty feet below, and a misstep could send one of them plunging to an awfully hard landing.

They made it about halfway across when they heard a sound from the opposite bank. It was voices, too soft to understand.

"Greetings," Regdar said. "We were dispatched by Klionne. Are you the Atupalan party?"

Four figures in armor stepped in front of the bridge. They weren't the party from Atupal but rather orcs, armed and ready for combat. The bridge shuddered under their additional weight.

Regdar unsheathed his greatsword, a long, thick weapon few men could handle. One of the orcs tossed a spear. It just missed Lidda, embedding in the side of the bridge behind her.

"You missed me, pig!" she shouted, flourishing her sword.

The orcs' response was a sharp battle cry as they charged. The bridge heaved and sagged under the pounding weight. Almost immediately a slat gave way beneath one of the orcs, who tumbled through to the river below. The ice shattered where he impacted. The others continued unperturbed.

Regdar was startled when he felt the quarrel from a crossbow zip past his head, almost striking his helmet. The bolt came from behind them. He whirled about to see six more orcs rushing onto the bridge from the other bank, their armor covered with snow. Another quarrel struck him in the chest but bounced harmlessly off the steel breast plate beneath his winter furs.

"Gods," he muttered under his breath. Those weren't boulders at all on the far side of the bridge but concealed orcs. He should have guessed.

"Are they crazy?" Lidda yelled. "They'll bring down the bridge and all of us with it!"

She slipped behind Regdar to face the orcs coming up

behind them. They looked crazy, their eyes glassed over with rage. Orcs weren't temperate beasts under any circumstance, and this unexpected event probably had them lashing out at anyone they could blame.

As the orcs drew close, Lidda used her lightness to her advantage by springing from her place and landing on the bridge's handrail. Her blade sliced an orc across its face. The orc squealed in pain and tripped backward. It broke through a portion of the far handrail as it tumbled off the bridge, joining its fellow in the ice below. Another swung its axe at Lidda, but she dodged the weapon easily and jumped behind the orcs this time. She heard wood breaking beneath her feet and barely pulled away before the deck gave way with a loud crack.

Meanwhile Regdar decided to do the last thing the orcs expected and meet their charge. He rushed headlong into the oncoming orcs, greatsword swinging. The sword struck a club from one of his opponent's hands, propelling it over the side of the bridge. The orc drew back in sudden fear. It tripped one of its fellows, who slipped on the icy wood and fell at Regdar's feet. The others trampled it as it tried futilely to pull itself up. The orc with the crossbow fired a second bolt at close range. Regdar barely managed to block it with the blade of his sword.

Lidda swore at the two orcs from the other side of the broken slat, trying everything to get them to step forward and risk falling into the river below. They resisted her taunts and turned instead on Regdar, running toward his unguarded back.

"Behind you!" Lidda shouted. The fighter replied with a horizontal swing of his greatsword as he pirouetted. The blade chopped through the handrail of the bridge on one side and caught both of the orcs in the midsection, slicing through their armor and drawing blood from their bellies.

They stumbled back wounded and with all their attention suddenly focused on the human. Lidda hopped over the broken slat to slit the throat of first one, then the other. With that, all the orcs attacking from the far side of the bridge were defeated, so she moved up to Regdar's side to face off against those remaining.

"Hey, friends!" came a voice from somewhere. "Are we too late to help?"

Before Regdar and Lidda could reply, they heard a sound like the whistling of wind and a loud detonation opposite the orcs. One of the orcs was blown off its feet from behind. As it tumbled forward, it narrowly missed crashing into Regdar before falling off the side of the bridge.

"Be careful," Regdar shouted, recovering his footing and trading parries with the remaining orcs. "If there are any snowy mounds over there they might just be . . ."

An orc war-cry filled the air, confirming Regdar's suspicions. He and Lidda carved through the remaining two orcs on the bridge. When the orcs fell, the human and halfling could see that three more figures had joined the fray on the riverbank. At least four more orcs had also emerged from hiding there. Two of them engaged one man who wore a red leather military uniform and fought with a sword and a large, square shield. A black-robed man with a short spear held back another orc. A third figure, dressed in white and whirring about like a snowstorm, was an indistinct blur confronting the orc farthest from the bridge.

Regdar and Lidda rushed forward, mindful of their footing on the treacherous bridge, past the bodies of what they took to be dead or unconscious orcs. As they passed one, however, the orc's eyes popped open and it slashed Regdar's leg with its sword, leaving a long, jagged wound. Regdar fell forward with all his weight. His face smashed through one of the uneven slats, and he found himself staring down into the icy river and the broken bodies of the fallen orcs. There were jagged, dark holes where tumbling bodies had smashed through the brittle surface. The edge of the broken slat sliced Regdar's cheek.

Lidda served the treacherous orc a swift thrust of her sword into its belly. She was helping Regdar to his feet when she saw the uniformed man on the river bank overwhelmed by his orc opponents. He was clearly inexperienced in this sort of fighting. He held his shield so far from his body that the one of the orcs easily wrenched it aside, allowing the other to slash the man's sword arm. His sword, still gripped by his forearm, fell to the ground and disappeared beneath the snow. Their position was marked by a bright splash of red blood.

The man with the short spear, whose black cloak fluttered dramatically as he leaped and hopped, abandoned the axe-wielding orc before him and rushed to his fellow's aid. One of the orcs had its back turned, and it was immediately speared through the neck. The counterattack was too late to save the uniformed man, however; he had already joined his severed arm in a spreading, red stain beneath the thick carpet of snow.

Regdar rose to his knees with Lidda's help, then clutched the handrail and pulled himself to his feet. He was clearly in pain from his wounded leg, but he hobbled toward the far side of the bridge nevertheless. Lidda and Regdar reached the opposite bank in time to see the cloaked man conjure a pellet of solid magic in his hand and launch it at the orc that stood over the slain man. Trailing green streamers of magic, it caught the orc squarely in the face and sent it tumbling down the riverbank onto the solid ice beyond. The orc he'd turned his back on was rushing forward, axe raised overhead. Lidda leveled her crossbow and squeezed the trigger.

The quarrel buried itself in the orc's side. The brute registered its pain with a toothy snarl but continued toward the magic-user. Alerted by the snarl, the wizard snatched back his short spear from the neck of the slain orc at his feet and spun toward the threat. His turn was too slow. With a swing of its axe, the orc knocked away the weapon before it was in position.

Regdar raised his greatsword, but his wound slowed him too much to reach the orc before it could strike.

With a sudden whirr of snow and a loud smashing noise, something hit hard on the orc's head. The beast dropped its weapon and fell, its skull crushed by a heavy club in the hands of a slender, young woman who looked too weak to wield so massive a weapon. Regdar stared at her. An eerie quiet settled onto the bridge and its bloodied mass of churned snow and crumpled bodies.

The woman's white robes were elegantly functional but far too sheer for this climate. Her face was what riveted Regdar's attention. The warrior was convinced he was looking at a creature from one of the goodly planes rather than this coarse world. She lowered her hood, displaying a short crop of honey-blond hair framing a pale, crystalline face that was smooth and pure. Regdar stared at her until Lidda tugged his arm, bringing him back into the world.

The man who had just been saved by the woman wrapped his arms around her. "You've saved me too many times now," he said. "I'll have to return the favor one of these days."

She spoke, and the sound was like the ringing of crystal. "If only we could have saved him." She looked down on the dead man, who Regdar and Lidda could see was little more than a boy in armor.

"What was his name?" asked Lidda.

"Teron. Teron of Atupal," this unearthly woman said. "He was one of the town guard. I suspect he lied to us when he claimed to be an experienced warrior."

"There aren't too many like him in Atupal," the man said.

He turned to Lidda and Regdar. "We should introduce ourselves. My name's Hennet Dragonborn." He gave a courtly smile to Lidda, striking an exaggerated pose as he did, with his shoulders back, head high, and one leg far ahead of the other. Lidda was charmed instantly, and Regdar was wary.

"It'll be nice to work with a wizard again," Lidda told him. "We haven't since . . ."

"Not a wizard, little miss," Hennet corrected, "but close. I'm a sorcerer. And if you like spellcasters, here's another for you. Let me present Sonja of the North."

"Another spellcaster?" asked Regdar, cocking an eye-brow. "Are you a priestess, milady?"

"No, not a priestess," she said with a slight laugh. "I'm a druid, but I can heal that gash in your leg, if you wish."

"A druid?" asked Lidda. "You don't look like any druid I've met." Most of them wore only green or brown, Lidda reflected, while Sonja looked as if she had been born in the snow.

"And you'll never find another like Sonja," Hennet said, running a hand over her back. "Her home is the northern tundra. Nightfall's coming. Let's make camp. We can explain more once we have some shelter."

"I trust you're the party from Atupal," said Regdar.

"Hired and dispatched by Atupal, yes," Hennet explained, "but not from Atupal. We were just there when this strange affair started. If that's what you're worried about, we have no particular stake in Atupal's relations with Klionne."

"Nor do we," said Lidda. "Klionne hired us to investigate this phenomenon, too. Don't get me wrong, we care about the people of Klionne. Just not . . ."

"Just not its petty squabbles with its neighbor," finished Hennet. He looked down at Teron's corpse. "He didn't care about those things, either. He begged us to let him come along. I think he hoped we'd adopt him or some such thing and invite him to go adventuring with us after this. So much for adventures." He turned to Sonja. "I suppose we'll have to pick up his body on the way back. The cold should keep it preserved well enough, if the wolves don't find it."

"I'm Regdar," the fighter interrupted, "and this is Lidda. This bridge was unstable before, and it's only gotten worse because of the fight. If we're careful, it may hold together."

They crossed the bridge one at a time. Hennet went first, poking each orc body with his spear to be sure it was dead before pushing it off the bridge with his foot. Reassembled on the far side, they finished their introductions.

"I hope we can trust your dedication to this mission," Sonja declared to Regdar and Lidda.

Lidda instantly gritted her teeth, bracing for Regdar's heated comeback. Instead, she was shocked to hear him say, "Of course." Instead of being insulted, Regdar smiled at the woman and looked every inch the fool.

"We're here to safeguard the lives of the people of Klionne and Atupal and all those beyond this region who may be affected by this phenomenon."

"The people should be protected, yes," the druid said, "but the damage is done already." She spread her arm to indicate the vast expanse of white surrounding them. "Human lives may be protected from the cold, but what of this? Animals, plants, the land itself, all these natural cycles have been hideously disrupted. This is not supposed to be. Some magic has made it this way, and it is my duty to undo it, or at least to minimize the damage. The cycle of nature is broken here, and it must be restored."

Regdar frowned slightly, but Lidda shook her head. If

this Sonja was like most of the druids she'd met, Lidda suspected that humanity was a distant second concern for her. Druids worried about nature first. But, Lidda supposed, the woman's motivation didn't really matter if she was willing to help them.

"I had to persuade the mayor of Atupal to let Sonja come on this mission," Hennet said. "The people there aren't all as friendly as Teron was. Half of them wanted to lock her up out of suspicion that she was responsible for this."

"I don't suppose you can control the weather?" Lidda asked this new companion.

"I'm afraid not," Sonja replied, "but I do know some spells that might make the cold a little easier to endure for you and the others."

Regdar smiled at her like a puppy.

"Uh, Regdar," said Hennet uncertainly, "why don't we compare maps and see what we can figure out about this region." He unfolded a parchment from his pocket. "The one they gave me in Atupal is pretty bare, and I feel lucky to have it. They weren't especially gracious or generous, considering we're going out to their rescue. Aside from some trinkets and the vague promise of riches on our return, all they gave us was this map, an old wand, and a magic ring for Sonja."

Hennet slid a wooden wand from his furs. It was about the length of a short sword—too long to carry in a pocket but easily thrust through a belt without being much of a hindrance. At first glance it looked like an ordinary piece of wood, but its gnarled tip resembled a flicker of flame that was so startlingly realistic it couldn't be a simple carving. It identified this device as a wand of fire or fireballs. Such a weapon could be very deadly, if used with care. From the way Hennet handled it, Lidda could see that he regarded the wand with a mix of awe and casual confidence.

"I doubt my map is much better than yours," Regdar said.

When he unfolded it next to Hennet's, everyone could see that both were equally barren of detail. Hennet wondered aloud, "How can these people live so close to this place but never visit it long enough even to make a map?"

"They fear it," answered Regdar, "probably with good reason. Tomorrow, we'll start toward this Fell Forest. The people in Klionne think the forest is the origin of this cold. That could be nothing more than local prejudice and superstition, but who knows? Maybe they're right."

Hennet nodded. "Sonja tried to dispel the wave when it passed over us. That ring the mayor gave her was supposed to do the trick, but it didn't even to slow the . . . whatever this is down."

"I had little hope it would succeed," Sonja said. "The magic affects a huge area of land, so its power must be far greater than anything in this ring. I had hoped, however, that I might slow it down, but there was no noticeable effect at all. The ring worked. I could feel it, and its magic was not insubstantial. But it was as if the power of this ring was inconsequential against the advancing wave of cold. Whatever drives this is operating with an entirely different magnitude of force."

"I don't follow you," Lidda injected. "You mean, it was like this cold just ignored your spell, as if it didn't exist?"

Sonja shook her head. "Many variables come into play when trying to cancel one magical effect with another, too many for me to say with certainty what really happened. It was . . . unusual, but I'm not sure why. In all likelihood, an effect this large was created by magic that's too advanced for this ring to dispel. That's not uncommon. Perhaps I'll have better luck at its source."

Talk about the impenetrability of this magic made Lidda uneasy, so she changed the subject. "What shall we do about the bridge?"

"What do you mean?" asked Hennet. "Why worry about the bridge?"

"Those orcs we fought were desperate. I don't think they were here waiting to ambush someone coming across the bridge. The normal bridge traffic won't be coming through until this situation is resolved.

"I think those orcs were guards," she continued. "They were here to hold the bridge and protect it from destruction so they could use it. Their homes are being wrecked and their routines disrupted by this cold. I'd bet they'll try to leave the area, and they'll cross this bridge to do it. When they do, they'll pose a danger to Atupal and Klionne. From what I've heard, they're not the only tribe of monsters out here. I say we should cut down the bridge."

Hennet's brow furrowed. "Then how will we get across the river on the way back?"

"If it gets warm again, we should be able to find a place to ford the river," answered Regdar. "If we can trust this thing they call a map, the river's somewhat narrower to the east."

Hennet shook his head firmly. "What if we need to leave in a hurry or before the river warms up? As you said, the bridge is barely standing now. If monsters try to use it, the whole thing will probably collapse under their feet. A few less orcs in the world is fine with me."

"That's beside the point," Regdar protested, but he was interrupted by Sonja.

"It's almost sundown, and while I can probably travel this terrain by night, I trust that isn't the case for the rest of you. We can worry about the bridge in the morning."

With a few quick spells, Sonja cleared an area of snow to pitch their tents. She shared a tent with Hennet and Lidda shared with Regdar. As Hennet kept watch outside, Regdar whispered to Lidda, "What do you think of Hennet?"

You don't want to know what I think, she thought, but all

she said was, "What kind of name is Hennet? Sounds like a chicken."

Regdar chuckled softly. The halfling whispered, "What do you think of Sonja?"

The fighter thought on that. "I don't know," he honestly said. She had healed his leg by running her palm over the wound, and she did it with the powers of nature, not the clerical magic he was more familiar with. It felt different; more organic, more personal. The contrast intrigued him, and so did Sonja.

The temperature dropped considerably overnight. In the morning, as they dismantled their camp, Lidda repeated her concerns about the bridge, seconded by Regdar. Only they favored destroying it, and with the vote split two and two, the bridge was allowed to stand.

"I make it about two days to the forest," Hennet announced after studying his map for a few minutes. "That's assuming we can keep moving as if this were summer . . . which, of course, it is." He paused for laughs that didn't come then pointed into the distance. "It's somewhere in this direction. And that's about all the information we're going to get from these maps. We can probably throw them away once we actually start moving."

"We might need them on the way back," Sonja reminded him.

"Yes," he allowed, "the way back. We certainly will want to be able to find our way back to Atupal and Klionne with the head of the dragon in tow so we can collect our rewards and be feted as heroes."

"Dragon!" shouted Lidda and Regdar in synch. "What dragon?"

"Oh," Sonja's face turned dour. "You hadn't heard?"

"Word must not have gotten to Klionne before you left," Hennet said. "The day before we set out, a traveler came into

Atupal saying he'd passed through a little hamlet called Litkil, north of the city. He found it empty, all the people dead—frozen, as if by a white dragon's breath. The hamlet was outside the cold zone at the time. The treasury and the local shrines were ransacked but the houses were otherwise undisturbed."

"You think a white dragon is causing this?" asked Regdar. "All this is about a dragon building a hoard?"

Hennet nodded. "It looks that way."

"The real question," Sonja said, "is where it came from. It's not likely that the dragon and the cold are a coincidence. White dragons don't come this far south. Mind you, neither do ice druids."

"A dragon," Lidda repeated. Monsters were plentiful, but a dragon . . . the mythic weight behind the word made her tremble in excitement and fear.

"Well, the sooner we get underway, the sooner we can slay it. This way." Hennet pointed toward the north and took one step before Regdar stopped him.

"It's not that way," Regdar corrected. "If I read the maps right, it's more . . . that way." He pointed slightly to the left of Hennet's direction.

"Oh, is it?" Hennet replied, suddenly belligerent. "I hoped it wouldn't come to this, but maybe before we go much farther we should choose a leader. In case squabbles like this break out, we should have somebody to solve them." He cast Regdar a sideways glance. "We ought not waste our efforts fighting each other."

"Right," Regdar answered. "Who shall it be? Atupal or Klionne?"

"Boys, boys," Lidda interjected. "If you're not too busy measuring your swords, let me suggest a solution. Let's make the leader the person who's most at home in this landscape, who has the most experience with snow, and who I'm guessing knows more about white dragons than anyone else here."

All eyes turned to Sonja, who beamed with a mix of modesty and pride. She pointed directly between Regdar and Hennet's points.

"This way," she said. That way they went.

It was several hours later when they first saw the dragon. It was hard to spot at first, because the wind had picked up and snow was shifting and blowing across the landscape. The movement caught Lidda's eye. It was little more than a white dot against the blue sky in the distance, but it was approaching fast. Immediately Sonja chanted a few exotic syllables, and the party felt magic enfold them.

"What have you done to us?" asked Regdar, holding up his hand to look at it. His skin and clothes were completely white so that he could barely be seen against the snowy background. He saw that the others were similarly changed. He could see them because of the textures of their clothing and their sharp outlines and because they were silhouetted against the horizon, but from overhead or with a white background they would be nearly invisible. Sonja shushed Regdar, and the four of them watched as the dragon turned in a wide circle then grew smaller in the distance.

Lidda ran her hand through her supplies, making sure she still had the potion of flight she'd picked up last month in the great city of Vasaria. It was an extravagant purchase, one she hadn't told Regdar about. She bought it for personal use, but now that a dragon was involved she decided to keep it closer at hand, in her vest pocket.

"I've never seen this spell before," said Regdar, inspecting his stark white shoulder closely.

"I call it snow shield," the druid answered. "My parents

developed it. Helps you disappear when a predator's approaching. Dragons have exceptionally good eyes. We're lucky it hadn't seen us already. Or, for that matter," she looked back behind them, "our tracks." Their footprints were only partially concealed by the blowing snow.

"A nice spell, but Sonja, why did you cast it?" complained Hennet. "Now the dragon's flying away and who knows when it might come back? With luck, I might still be able to get its attention. If we bring it close, we can finish it here and now. I could use this fireball wand, or you could use that new lightning trick of yours. I've been dying to see that."

"I can only do that in a storm," Sonja said, "and I wouldn't have anyway. If we tried to fight the creature now, the dragon would fly right over us, swoop down, and freeze us with its breath before we could touch it. Have you felt a white dragon's breath? It can freeze your flesh solid, cocoon you in ice. Even a young one can do that. This isn't the right time. When we face the dragon, we need to do it on our terms, where we'll stand a chance. "

"But the dragon was flying in the direction of Atupal," Hennet protested. "If it hadn't turned, our inaction might have cost lives."

"If it hadn't turned, any action would have cost our lives, and then the dragon could have flown on to Atupal anyway," the druid shot back. "Would that be better?"

If they were a romantic couple, Regdar reflected, they weren't yet in synch.

As if on cue, the spell expired, and Hennet and Sonja's spat abated with it. The cold march continued across the snowfields.

Near midday, Hennet and Regdar moved into some brush to set a snare, hoping to catch a few rabbits for their next meal. Lidda and Sonja rested against a rock that sheltered them from the wind and listened to the two men arguing in the distance.

"Isn't this place," Lidda asked, "this kind of landscape, like where you come from?"

"In some ways," Sonja said with a touch of sadness. "If I were to let that part of me come to the fore, I would feel quite at home here. But this is an abomination. It's unnatural, and that makes it very different from my home."

"Why did you leave there?" Lidda probed.

Sonja smiled at the halfling, a smile so benevolent that even Lidda felt its attraction. It was no wonder men responded so favorably to Sonja. There was bottomless warmth to her smile, Lidda thought. Such strange beauty— her cheeks registered as much warmth as an ice sculpture. Lidda wondered if Sonja might have some elf blood in her. She knew that in druid communities, race played little part in relationships. Elf heritage would go a long way toward explaining her otherworldly looks and the quiet, unconscious sensuality in her every movement. In that way, Sonja was much like Regdar's beloved Naull, who had been taken from him only a few months ago.

Lidda had been carefully observing Regdar's reactions to Sonja. She knew that in his heart he was loyal to Naull and that he believed she still lived somewhere in captivity, but Sonja must seem very appealing to him in his loss. Her most arresting quality was her serenity. Despite the strong, measured passion she displayed, she was an island of peace in all of this chaos. For men of violence, and for Regdar especially, she must seem like shelter from the storm.

"I was fifteen years old before I saw a human being other than my parents," Sonja explained. "They were members of a druidic circle in one of the great southern forests, but they decided to put the druidic community behind them to pursue unity with nature and their own interests. They resolved to go to the place farthest removed from man that they could find, just the way the great druids of history did. So they departed for the far north." A faraway smile crossed Sonja's face as she thought of her birthplace.

"I was born in the shadow of the Endless Glacier, along the ever-white valleys and ridges that surround it, where they made their home. There were wars to fight there too, against the evil frost giants who rule the tundra like tyrants, bringing white dragons and verbeegs and winter wolves and a dozen other races under their control. Mostly my parents just tended to the animals and plants and to the ice itself. In time their skills became atuned to this landscape. They raised me as a druid and taught me those same skills."

"What happened?" asked Lidda. "Why did you leave?"

"I left when my parents died. It was nothing heroic. The tundra takes its toll even on ice druids. They and I still had relatives in the southlands, farmers and even city-dwellers who never understood their decision to leave. Before they died they made me promise to travel south and visit those relatives and former friends, to explain to them what they had done with their lives and why. Looking back on it now, I think they sent me south because they didn't want me to live a solitary life in the bitter cold just because they did. They wanted me to see some of the world so that I could choose my own home."

"What choice will you make?"

"I met my parents' family," Sonja went on. "They were warm to me, but they could not understand me. No one can."

"Not even Hennet?" asked Lidda. Sonja shook her head, smiling sadly.

"So then," Lidda said, "you intend to return?"

"I intend to," Sonja replied. "It has been a long time, though. Too long, I feel." She gestured around her. "All of this is very familiar to me and welcoming. I miss it greatly. I didn't realize until now how much I missed it, or how my abilities have lain fallow in the south. When I was twelve, I would never have been surprised by orcs concealed under mounds of snow."

"Where did you meet Hennet?" Lidda continued. "What's his story?"

"I fear that Hennet's story changes every time he tells it," Sonja laughed, and the sound was like sun sparkling on icicles. "In the southlands I discovered something my parents never explained to me. I met men my age and found that they could . . . satisfy certain needs."

"Happens to the best of us," Lidda said with a bawdy wink. "I don't suppose there was much of that type of action up in the arctic, was there?"

"I should say not," the druid responded with a smile. "I met him at a ducal ball. Hennet is handsome, dashing. He's a little . . ."

"Enamored of himself?" offered Lidda.

"He's not entirely as charming as he thinks," Sonja said, "yet that only makes him even more charming, in a sweet way. Someone close to him recently left him, and he was looking for comfort. I was looking for a traveling companion. It was a good fit, convenient for us both. I don't expect too much of him, and he doesn't expect too much of me."

"That simple, is it?" asked Lidda warily.

"Not quite," Sonja admitted, looking the halfling squarely in the eye. "You and Regdar are born adventurers, and so is Hennet. You're well suited to this rootless life. If my time with Hennet has taught me one thing, it is that I am not. I've learned that staying in one place is very important to me."

Before Lidda could blurt out another question, Hennet and Regdar returned empty-handed. Lidda was filled with questions, but the conversation would have to wait for later.

The wind was increasing slowly but steadily, and stinging ice crystals occasionally whipped around their sheltering rock to bite the halfling's cheek. She pulled her fur-lined hood tighter around her neck.

"Sonja," Lidda asked, "can it get much colder than this?"

Sonja gazed off at the horizon, barely visible through a stormy, white haze blanketing the formerly blue sky.

"It can," she said, "and it will."

As the day went on, the sky grew whiter and whiter and the wind more chill. Hennet watched the horizon vanish and the last patch of blue disappear from the sky and wondered for an awful moment if they'd ever see sun or sky again. Then the snow came, gently at first, ethereal snowflakes that Lidda liked to catch on her tongue, followed by a steady fall of fat flakes that impeded visibility. Regdar and Hennet hunted for food on the march, hoping to stretch their rations while hunting was still possible, but they could not manage any catches. Sonja solved this. She stood still and closed her eyes, and in time a furry, brown rabbit hopped out of a gully toward her. Lidda cooed over it as it poked its head up and wiggled its pink nose. Sonja took it in her hands and calmly snapped its neck.

"Here is our meal," she said.

The others looked at her with open-mouthed shock. "Why did you do that?" asked Regdar.

"Weren't you hungry?" she asked. No one said anything more about it.

Some time later, the party came across tracks for the first time. These were not human tracks but something larger. Lidda inspected them closely.

"Gnolls?" she asked.

Sonja nodded gravely.

"We knew humanoid tribes lived in this area," said Regdar. "We can't expect them to be huddling in a cave somewhere. Gnolls are strong and don't care much about the cold."

"Their life has been disrupted," added Sonja. "They'll be on the ready, too, and rightly so."

"Great!" Hennet rubbed his brow. "This snow stirs up the gnolls, and they'll blame the first outsiders they see."

"And these footprints are fresh," Lidda said, watching the snowflakes fall. "Old tracks wouldn't last long under these conditions."

The travelers immediately silenced themselves and surveyed their surroundings. Dimly in the snow they could make out two large, brown-black forms moving quickly. One moved silently toward them, a battle-axe in its hands, but the other was running away. There could be only one reason such a sturdy and warlike humanoid would flee from a fight.

"It'll warn their tribe!" yelled Regdar. He strung his longbow with stiff fingers as Lidda pulled out her crossbow and cocked it. Both fired at nearly the same time, but aiming was difficult through the snowy haze. Hennet readied a magic missile. A tiny bolt of magic blasted from his palm, bathing the plain in a sickly, green glow for a few thrilling moments. It flew unerringly to its target and struck the gnoll in the leg, toppling it to the ground. By then, the other one was lost in the snow and haze.

"That's all we need," Hennet cursed as they rushed to the fallen gnoll. "Now we can expect a gnoll tribe down on our heads."

The stricken gnoll wasn't dead. It lay sprawled out on the

ice with its axe inches beyond its desperately groping fingers. Regdar shoved the weapon away with his toe. The gnoll spat at them and swore in its native language until Regdar kicked its wounded leg. That brought a yip to its canine jaws, but the next time it spoke, it used uncertain Common.

"It was yoouuu!" The gnoll gasped. "You destroyed our homes, killed our young!"

"Your home," said Sonja. Even for this beast the concern in her voice was genuine. "Where was your home?"

"The wood! Our forest is no more. This plague of ice has destroyed it. We flee, but your ice is too fast. We die! You kill us!"

"We didn't destroy your homes," said Regdar. "We're here to stop this ice."

"Lies! Lies!" the gnoll howled. It lunged for Lidda's throat, no doubt deciding the halfling would be the easiest to kill before the larger humans could slay it. It was wrong, as Lidda proved with a quick jab of her sword. The creature fell back into the snow and lay still.

A deep-toned, throaty horn sounded in the distance. Sonja readied her club.

"They won't listen to reason," the druid said. "I recommend you put away your bows. Under these conditions, they will be on us before we know it. We have an advantage, though. There's still a lot of glare coming off the snow. Gnolls dislike bright light. It hurts their eyes and impairs their fighting ability."

Little more than a minute passed before the gnolls came into view. Their tall, brown forms were silhouetted against the whiteness of the background. Eight or nine of them emerged from the swirling snow. Their hyenalike heads towered far above the humans. They fanned out quickly so that their foes were surrounded inside a widely spaced ring. They were armed with a hodgepodge of weapons, and some of them wore mismatched pieces of armor. One, swinging a flail, wore a coal-black breastplate emblazoned with the emblem of the god Erythnul. The breastplate was human-sized and too small for a gnoll; undoubtedly it was a trophy. This gnoll was slightly smaller than the others and kept behind them as the ring closed in on the party.

As the gnolls drew nearly within striking range, Lidda rushed forward, bobbing between their legs to confound their attempts to attack her with their axes. Wherever she passed, she slashed at the gnolls' shins and knees. Her hit-and-run attacks so angered her victims that three of them broke ranks and chased after her. By doing so, they exposed their flanks. The advantage was momentary, but Regdar, an experienced warrior who'd fought alongside Lidda before, was ready for it. The instant the first gnoll turned, the armored human lunged forward. The gleaming tip of his greatsword was just as deadly as the edge, and a straight thrust through the creature's ribs slew it on its feet. A second gnoll was sliced down before the others realized what was happening. Yips and howls filled the air as the monsters reacted and warned each other of the fast-moving danger. The encircling gnolls leaped back several steps, widening the gaps between them, and ignored Lidda. Their attention was now riveted on the fur-wrapped man with the steaming, red-stained sword.

Hennet held back for a moment, both to ready his spells and because he wasn't sure what the big man would do next.

Sonja slipped farther from Hennet. She knew that gnolls preferred to fight enemies who were separated from help, and she hoped that her move might lure a gnoll to closer range. It did. She tried to keep herself looking small and held her weapon uncertainly, like a frightened animal. Sensing an easy target, the gnoll rushed her, straight into the trap Sonja had laid for it. The ground beneath it was slick with magical ice, and the gnoll's feet slid out from underneath it. When it tumbled onto its back, its armor snapped under its weight with a sharp crack. Sonja jumped forward onto the momentarily stunned gnoll. She smashed her cudgel onto its skull with surprising force and instantly prepared to deliver a second blow, but when she pulled back the weapon she saw that the creature was already dead.

The gnolls were bloodied but not defeated. The survivors circled and regrouped and forced Regdar, Hennet, and Sonja again into the center of a circle, smaller than the first. Lidda bobbed around the outside, sneaking in with her short sword to nick their flanks and keep them distracted, then skittering away whenever one turned to attack her. The smaller gnoll with the breastplate still held back from the action, and Lidda suddenly realized why. The emblem of Erythnul on its armor was not just for show.

"It's casting!" Lidda yelled. She pulled out her crossbow, desperate to distract the gnoll before it could complete its spell. She was too late, and worse, she was the spell's target. Lidda found herself paralyzed, her limbs locked in place like a statue's. She could breathe and move her eyes but couldn't move or run—or speak. She watched as the gnoll priest closed in on her, its flail waving high above its head. Her mouth was locked open in a silent scream.

"Protect Lidda!" Hennet shouted. He rushed toward her and launched a magic missile at the gnoll priest. It impacted against the breastplate but seemed to do no real damage. The energy was dissipated by the apparently magical piece of armor. The priest responded by turning to Hennet and mumbling another spell. A new weapon suddenly appeared in its outstretched hand, a morning star with a solid head made of stone.

The corner of the gnoll priest's snout rose in something like a smile as the morning star flew from its hand toward

Hennet and soundly whacked the sorcerer on his shoulder. The blow took Hennet by surprise and knocked him off balance. Then the morning star struck again, moving like a blur. It caught Hennet along his side, knocking him to the snowy ground. As Hennet fumbled for his spear or spells, the magical morning star pummeled him ruthlessly. He rolled onto his back with his short spear in his hands and tried to defend himself, but the flying weapon was virtually impossible to parry as it swooped from side to side.

Regdar and Sonja slashed and bullied their way through the other gnolls in their effort to reach Lidda, who was completely at the gnoll priest's mercy. Sonja leaped at the tall monster with her left hand held before her. When it passed before the gnoll's face, it erupted with a brilliant flash of white. The blinded gnoll fell back away from Sonja's flare, dazzled and incapacitated.

Sonja bashed the flail from the gnoll's hand with her cudgel. Regdar stepped next to her and thrust his greatsword into the creature's chest. The sword struck against Erthynul's breastplate, which wasn't even dented by the full force of Regdar's strength. The breastplate, however, was designed for a human and not a gnoll. Regdar easily redirected the blade to an unprotected spot. The greatsword sliced through the gnoll's hide, and blood gushed down the blade. The gnoll cried out in a fruitless prayer to its god, concluding with a piercing, canine shriek when Regdar twisted the wide blade between its ribs. The gnoll slid off the steel and fell back, the agonized look of the abandoned faithful forever frozen on its hairy face.

Hennet twisted and slashed with his spear in a desperate attempt to deflect the magical morning star's next assault, when the weapon pulled back and vanished. Breathing a sigh of relief and using his short spear for leverage, he rose onto his feet. Other gnolls still circled uncertainly, and Hennet thrust the spear before him to keep them at a distance.

Regdar wasn't interested in keeping a distance. With the sorcerer defending himself, the easiest victim for the bloodthirsty gnolls was the paralyzed halfling. The gnolls closed in on Lidda and almost reached her when Regdar assaulted them, jumping straight into their midst.

Two gnolls died instantly when Regdar clove through them at waist height with a single, powerful swing of his weapon. A third gnoll would have joined them, but it managed to block Regdar's blade with the head of its axe. Gore splattered off Regdar's sword onto the creature. The gnoll, rather than trying to riposte with its ringing axe, let the weapon fall to the ground. It boldly grasped Regdar's blade with its two bare hands. Blood rolled along the sword's length and dripped onto the snow as the gnoll squeezed and pulled. With its great strength, it wrenched the bloody greatsword from Regdar's grasp.

The gnoll hurled the heavy weapon far across the snow, yelping as the edge cut deeper into its palms. Regdar, weaponless but not helpless, drove a fist into the gnoll's throat. The gnoll lurched backward, trying to defend itself with its bleeding hands. Regdar responded by kicking its armored belly, knocking the gnoll onto its back. He was about to reclaim his greatsword when the other gnolls attacked him from behind.

A studded mace struck Regdar's left shoulder, cracking the bone. Regdar whirled about to face the attacker and tried to punch the gnoll, but it caught his fist in its free hand and twisted. The pain dropped the fighter to his knees. Another of the beasts wrapped its long fingers around Regdar's neck and squeezed, emitting a snarl of victory as it did so. A third gnoll pinned Regdar's struggling hands and arms from behind. Regdar would have screamed from the pain in his shoulder, but the grip on his neck was too tight. The human gulped desperately for air, neck muscles straining to keep his windpipe open.

Relief came when Hennet's spell hit the gnoll that was strangling Regdar. The gnoll released its grip and stumbled back in time for another missile to catch it mid stride. The creature's smoking corpse collapsed at Regdar's feet.

The gnoll with the studded mace raised the weapon to smash Regdar's skull, but Sonja stepped behind it and snapped its knee with a well-placed blow from her cudgel. The monster tumbled backward, and the cudgel cracked its forehead on the way down. The gnoll that held Regdar by the arms pulled away immediately, letting Regdar's inert form collapse to the ground. Near panic, it fled directly toward Hennet and his short spear. The gnoll dodged and twisted past the sorcerer. Hennet turned and tossed the spear, hitting the gnoll in the back and bringing it down. The sorcerer ran and yanked his weapon from the living flesh then drove it hard into the fallen gnoll's outstretched neck.

Moments later, the spell that held Lidda wore off, and she suddenly finished cocking her crossbow with a lurch.

"I missed the battle," she lamented. "I didn't do you any good."

"Don't blame yourself for that," Hennet told her. "It could have happened to any one of us."

Lidda turned around and surveyed the carnage that lay all about the snowy, bloodstained field. Regdar was sprawled across the corpses of two gnolls with Sonja kneeling at his side and grasping his wrist.

"Will he be all right?" Lidda asked, the worry clear in her voice.

"I think so," the druid replied, though there was uncertainty on her face, "but I have much work to do."

They pitched the tents early. Hennet, wounded by the gnoll priest's spiritual weapon, rested in a tent with Lidda while Sonja worked her spells on Regdar in the other. Sonja needed a certain amount of quiet for her spells to work. They only hoped that their fire wouldn't attract unwanted attention from gnolls or anything else. In their favor was the near-white out condition. Between the haze and blowing snow, visibility was almost gone. It was only Sonja's excellent sense of direction that would keep them on the right path from that point on.

Lidda was cleaning the crusted gnoll blood from Regdar's greatsword when Hennet asked, "How long have you known Regdar?"

"Quite a while," Lidda said, looking up from the sword. "We were both fledgling adventurers when we first met. I was having some problems with the militia in a small town. Regdar and another friend, a priest named Jozan, helped me out. He saved my life, but don't tell him I said so."

"Then you owe Regdar," Hennet suggested. "Do you travel with him out of obligation?"

"Not at all. I travel with him because I like him. Everyone becomes his friend in time. You will too; there's no reason you shouldn't. He's not as immediately likeable these days as he once was. Lately," she confessed, "I've been concerned about him. He's not the same as he was when we first met."

"I've been meaning to ask you something," Hennet said. "An indelicate question, to be sure . . ."

"Could that be," Lidda responded, "what's with him? Why is he so abrupt? Doesn't he ever say 'please'? Is he always like that?"

"I would have put it more diplomatically," said Hennet, "but yes."

Lidda considered before answering. "He can't be with somebody he loves."

"I know how that feels."

"But you're with the person you love," she said, pointing to Sonja's tent through the snow. Hennet twitched.

"Sonja, yes, but in the past it's happened that . . ." Hennet trailed off, suddenly unsure of how to finish his sentence. He changed the subject. "Does Regdar always fight so rashly, rushing into danger like that? I'm surprised he's lived this long."

"No," Lidda replied. "That's something new since Naull disappeared. I'm worried about him. Naull's disappearance has had a real effect on him, that's for sure. I guess he feels disconnected from other people, even me. I'm worried this behavior might get really get him hurt."

"You say I'll get to like him in the end?" asked Hennet.

"I guarantee it," said Lidda with a smile.

"Say," said Hennet, "we've discussed the romantic status of the rest of our little party. What about you?"

This surprised Lidda. Her stature often made humans, Regdar included, forget that she was an adult woman. For Hennet to bring it up now touched her greatly.

"Most of the men I meet are just a little too tall for me,"

she said. "Really, they couldn't even kiss me without making themselves look ridiculous. But if you should happen to know any available men of any race who happen to be under four feet tall . . ."

Their laughter echoed across the stark white landscape.

Across the camp in the other tent, Regdar awoke from the magically induced sleep Sonja had placed on him. His eyes crept open and beheld the face of an angelic being of light. The wind outside howled threateningly, but Regdar felt safe and sheltered from the storm. Sonja's once-immaculate white robes were splattered with bloodstains, but this did little to diminish the feeling of peace she inspired in Regdar. Her smooth, white features, her smile, open yet mysterious . . . he was enraptured. Never, not even at their tenderest moment, had he seen Naull the way he was seeing Sonja now—healer, druid, warrior, angel.

"Welcome back, Regdar," she said. "That was some fight."

"Yes, it was," the fighter replied. "Is everyone all right? How's Lidda?"

"Safe. Uninjured. Hennet took a few thumps from the gnoll priest's magical morning star, but he's fine now, too."

Regdar ran his hand over his neck and shoulder. The pain was nearly gone. "My sword?" he asked.

"We have it. You know, Regdar, if you keep fighting like that, you might find yourself beyond all my spells next time."

"They would have killed Lidda," he explained. "She was helpless. I did what needed to be done."

"I know, Regdar, I know, but in the future, please, an ounce of caution." She smiled down at him, and he gave up all resistance.

Her hand was on his chest. Regdar felt close to her indeed.

This was the first time they'd been together away from Hennet. He felt a warm rush of embarrassment. When Jozan healed him all those times, it was a quick, dutiful thing, then it was back to the fray. Now, supine and incapacitated under Sonja's tender care, he felt his cheeks burn red.

Part of him liked it quite a lot.

When Sonja healed his leg at the bridge, Regdar thought that it felt different from ordinary healing, more personal somehow. Now he was sure of it. In a way that was hard to express, he felt Sonja must have put something of herself into him. The closeness of it touched him deeply.

"We should get going," Regdar said, reaching for his armor only to cringe at a lingering pain in his shoulder.

"No you don't," said Sonja, gently pushing him down. "It's getting dark. We're here for the night. The Fell Forest isn't far off, if Hennet reads the maps right. Tomorrow we should reach what I think is the center of this cold zone. There we should find whatever brought on this 'plague of ice,' as the gnoll called it. I like its turn of phrase. It suggests contagion."

Something sank inside Regdar, and he felt a profound insignificance amid the scope of this crisis.

"Sonja, let me ask you something."

"Anything."

"Before we met on Berron Bridge, Lidda asked me about something she called an ice age. Sages say that this whole world was covered in ice in ancient times. She wondered if this was the same thing happening all over again. I didn't think so at the time, but now I'm starting to wonder. I don't know what to think. Is this some sort of replay of the distant past? The beginning of a new ice age?"

"I'm not a sage," Sonja responded, "and I don't know much more about ancient times than you. Maybe the world was covered in ice during some forgotten era. If it was, I promise you, it was a natural phenemon. I do know that nature is a pendulum. Sometimes it swings toward chaos and evil, sometimes toward order and goodness. It could just as easily fluctuate between heat and cold. But what's beyond these tent walls is not natural. It offends nature, and it offends me.

The druid reflected for a few moments before continuing. "Can I share something with you? It's something I haven't shown the others yet. I'm afraid it might unnerve them. I don't want to alarm them with something that I don't entirely understand myself."

Regdar nodded eagerly.

"I discovered this earlier." She reached beneath her robe and pulled out a small, delicate flower, cold violet in color.

"What is it?" asked Regdar.

"Cryotallis. When I was a little girl I called them 'snow-blooms' and never picked them. I found it poking its sad head over the layer of snow, just as snowblooms always do."

"What's the problem?" the warrior asked.

"Snowbloom grows where I came from, in the glacial lands of the far north. It does not grow here. It cannot. Furthermore—" she looked at the little blossom— "this flower shows weeks of growth. The cold zone was not at this extent weeks ago. This flower should not be here."

A chill passed between the druid and the fighter. He did not have to ask her the implications of this. He understood them all too well.

Truly, foul magic was at work.

The wind came up in the night, howling across the snowy plains, a mournful noise like the earth itself crying out in pain. The thin felt of the tents proved woefully inadequate against the snow, so the travelers abandoned them. They turned the tents into a windbreak and huddled around the fire for warmth, keeping a watch while trying desperately to get some sleep. Adventurers learned to sleep through such distractions, but this night, it proved nearly impossible. The snow piled so thick that it threatened to bury them. Only Regdar slept well, probably owing to Sonja's spells. He lay still the entire night, neither tossing nor turning, though Lidda was sure that at one point he uttered the name "Naull."

"If we died out here," Hennet whispered to whoever else might still be awake, "do you think anybody would ever find our corpses?"

"Maybe someday they'll thaw our bodies out of a block of solid ice," said Lidda. "The sages of the future will put us on display in their studies. We'll be their only proof of life before the 'big freeze'."

"Is that's what happening here?" Hennet asked. "The freezing of the entire world? The death of mankind?"

"And halfling kind," added Lidda. "Not to mention gnomes and elves. Dwarves might be all right, what with . . ."

"No." The interjection came from Sonja. "Life will survive, even if civilization dies."

"Sure," joked Hennet. "We can all become mammoth herders."

"Believe it," said Sonja. "Humans can adapt to living in almost anything, including this kind of cold. My parents did it. Others can do it."

"Untold thousands will die," protested Lidda.

"And their offspring will never know a world but this. They will be hardened stock, and they will endure. When I visited the druid circle to which my parents once belonged in the great southern forests, I met some druids who prayed for just such a disaster to come along to remove the blight of civilization and return mankind to the level of nature."

"Good to know somebody's happy about this," Hennet said, his voice thick with disgust.

"Not this," answered Sonja. "This is not nature."

"So you keep saying," asked Lidda, "but how can you know?"

"Yes," asked Hennet. "Not that I don't trust your instincts in this matter, but how can you tell this is some magical abomination and not some cruel quirk of nature?"

"I can't explain how I know," said Sonja, "but I do know." This she said with such conviction nobody questioned her further.

The three of them tried fruitlessly to get back to sleep.

At length, Lidda spoke again. She wasn't sure how much time had passed, but the cold sun was creeping over the horizon, and the fire was burned down to coals.

"Do you know who this benefits?" she asked. "White dragons. I bet our big, white friend out there is behind all of this."

"What do you think, Sonja?" said Hennet. "Is it possible?"

The druid shrugged. "White dragons are dangerous enemies, vicious and unpredictable. Some of them bury themselves in their lairs for centuries on end, caring for nothing but their hoards. I once watched a single white dragon slave rear back and destroy a half-dozen of its frost giant masters when one of them kicked it. But they're not known as planners. To be responsible for this, that white dragon would have to be far more intelligent than average. Or it had help."

Over the roar of the wind came a new sound, a distant, high-pitched howl. Hennet started. "What was that?"

"Probably nothing to worry about," said Sonja. "Just a wolf."

"Nothing else is normal here," Hennet said. "Why should the wolves be?" Already he was out from under his wool blankets and preparing himself for battle. This roused Regdar, who poked his head out, scratching his forehead.

"What's going on?"

"The mighty sorcerer heard a wolf," Lidda joked.

"Is that all?" asked Regdar and put his head down again.

"Now you laugh," said Hennet, "but we've seen the way nature is being stirred up. We don't know how a wolf would react to us."

"I wouldn't worry," said Sonja. "I have a certain way with wolves."

"There they are now," said Hennet. Gray and black forms stalked through the white haze, their wiry legs pacing through the snow, some with their muzzles lowered to the ground and sniffing for new scents. They were fairly close but seemed to be keeping their distance. One looked over at the party, giving them only a quick glance before looking away.

"Quick, let's move," said Sonja. Her voice was calm but urgent. "We're not far from those gnoll bodies. The wolves probably picked up the scent and are here to scavenge them. It's best we leave now."

In record time they dismantled their camp and were ready to move. They plodded through the deep snow under Sonja's leadership, leaving the wolves far behind.

"You're sure we're going the right direction?" asked Lidda. "We can't see the forest or the mountains anymore, so how can you be sure we're headed toward the Fell Forest?"

"You'll have to trust me on this," answered Sonja. "My direction sense is good, even in a blizzard."

"We don't have much choice," said Lidda. "If we're going to move at all, someone needs to pick a way."

High above, the sun inched across the sky, a bright spot plastered onto the cotton clouds. The wolf howls kept up from behind, seemingly drawing closer. One wolf followed them, and Sonja couldn't explain why. If the pack was feeding on the gnoll corpses, why would one shadow them? Though Sonja said nothing, her expression became more puzzled as the hours went by. In time they reached a set of low, snow-covered hills.

"These weren't marked on my map," said Regdar.

"Nor mine," Hennet agreed. "I'll have to share some strong words with the mapmaker when we get back. Assuming he's still alive."

"Can we go around?" asked Regdar.

"We might waste more time doing that than going straight across," Sonja said. "There may be valleys we could get through more quickly than traipsing over every hill. Let's spend some time seeking them out."

The occasional, eerie, wolf howl in the distance broke the silence.

"Something's not right," Sonja said. "Something's stirring them up and it's not just the weather."

When the wolves howled to the south, the marchers

veered north. When they heard wolves howling in the west, they turned east. Soon they found themselves hopelessly off track so that even Sonja's vaunted sense of direction seemed to be confounded. The clouds were so thick that no sign could be seen of the sun itself, not even a brighter portion of the sky. All was uniform and gray.

"Maybe we should stop avoiding these wolves," suggested Hennet. "They'll move if we come too near, won't they?"

"Normally, they would," agreed Sonja, "but I don't want to risk it. I suspect they're under outside influence of some kind. I don't know what it is. Maybe a lycanthrope or a vampire that has influence over wolves. Maybe something else. In any case, I don't want to face a whole wolf pack in this terrain and after yesterday's fight."

So they trudged on, weaving from east to west, until their path led them over a low ridge and the valley they sought opened before them.

"Let's hurry," Sonja advised. "I'll be happy to put these wolves behind me."

The floor of the valley was deep with snow, almost up to their knees, and the surrounding hills channeled the wind so blowing snow constantly pelted their faces. Still, the level ground was easier going than hiking across the ridges. The farther they went, the more jagged, rocky, and rugged the hills around them became. Sheer cliffs lined the valley walls. Occasionally these were cut by snow-drifted ravines. At points it ceased to be a valley so much as a canyon that twisted and wound its way through the hills, but mostly proceeded in what Sonja assured them was still the proper direction.

"I hope we reach the Fell Forest soon," said Hennet. He spoke softly, for Sonja warned them that loud noises might set off snowfalls. "I don't like it that we haven't seen any trees yet."

"You know what I don't like?" said Regdar. "No more wolves howling." The fighter forced a half-hearted smile. "I didn't like it when we could hear them, and I really don't like it now that we can't."

Soon, a straight, sharp, white cliff face loomed ahead of them, flanked on both sides by similarly unscalable bluffs. They turned back to find a ravine up which they could escape, and immediately the air was filled with lupine howls.

"They herded us in here, the damned beasts!" shouted Lidda, drawing her blade.

"It cannot be," said Sonja. "This isn't wolf behavior at all."

Slender, black forms appeared in the distance, running hard toward the small group, leaping and bounding through snow sometimes as deep as their heads. At least two dozen wolves could be seen, and maybe more behind.

"What do we do, Sonja?" asked Hennet.

"I could try to tame them with my spells, but I couldn't get them all. My magic might not function correctly, or at all, if something's at work in their minds." She breathed heavily, reluctant to say what she was thinking. "Bury them. Do it quickly and painlessly and hopefully we can escape before more arrive."

"Bury them?" said Hennet. Then he realized what she meant. The wolves were close now, only a dozen yards away. Their reddish eyes shone through the snow falling all around them, their jaws hung wide open, and drool dripped off their lolling, pink tongues. Hennet extended his hand toward a snowy patch along a cliff face overhanging the valley. He conjured a magic missile and fired it, striking the snow and sending a rumble echoing through the valley.

The ice slid down the side of the cliff like a long, solid sheet, leaving the open rock behind it. The avalanche struck the ground just before the wolf pack, kicking up a cloud of ice and snow that set the ice tumbling off the opposite cliff as well. A few defiant half-barks, half-howls could be heard through the rumbling of the cascading snow. Hennet's avalanche also tipped off lesser falls of snow all along the sides of the valley, almost reaching the party's position, but these were small and inconsequential. By the time the cloud of snow had settled enough to allow some visibility, the entire wolf pack was buried beneath the avalanche.

"That was unfortunate," said Sonja, her eyes lowered. Howls could still be heard in the distance. "Quick," she continued. "It sounds like the rest of the pack is in the valley already. We have to find a way out of here before they arrive."

The party carefully climbed over the mound of snow where the wolves were buried, falling leg-deep into the loose-packed snow as they did. The jumble filled the center of the valley, and they stuck to the walls as much as possible as they slid through to the other side.

It was hardest for Lidda, whose small legs barely lifted her above the level of the snow. As she clawed her way through, her leg brushed against something furry and dead within the mound. She clenched her teeth, trying not to think about it. When she made it to the other side, she was about to say something when a sudden stir of snow and teeth thrust out of the snow pile behind her, nudging against her leg.

Lidda let out a sharp yelp, sending a few trickles of snow from the unstable cliffs around them, and pulled away. A wolf's snow-covered snout poked out of the snow behind her, teeth bared and emitting a low growl. It didn't sink its teeth into Lidda's leg but offered only a small nip. Lidda spun around and drew her sword.

"Lidda, don't," said Sonja. "It could have bitten you but it didn't." The druid stepped forward as the weak and dying animal pulled more of its body out of the snow. Sonja helped it by grasping the scruff of its neck and hoisting it free. It lay on the ground, its stomach heaving.

"Uh, Sonja," said Hennet, "shouldn't we keep moving..."

Ignoring him, Sonja laid her hand over the wolf's head, stroking its ears gently, and she closed her eyes. A calmness overtook the animal's face, the redness clouding its eyes fading away. The wolf's mouth opened, and it let out a soft moan. Its eyes slipped shut, and the heaving of its chest ceased.

"Is it dead?" asked Lidda.

"It said something to me before it died," said Sonja. "It said 'don't resist.'"

"What does that mean?" asked Regdar.

The sound of running paws grew through the valley. This second wolf pack rounded a corner, coming into full view as it ran toward the party. There were many more of them in this group, so many that there was scarcely room enough for all of them in the valley. Regdar extended his hand to fire a magic missile, but Sonja pulled his arm back.

"That's not necessary," she said. "These wolves will not harm us."

"Are you kidding?" said Lidda, her sword at the ready.

"I'm serious. They were told not to kill us, and they won't. You selected me as your leader, so let me lead you now."

"Sonja," said Regdar, his hand on the hilt of his greatsword as the tide of wolves narrowed in, "are you absolutely sure?"

Sonja didn't answer but stared steel-eyed into the coming wolf pack. She raised her hands above her shoulders in a gesture of surrender.

When the wolves arrived, the pack did exactly as Sonja said. Some of them stopped in their tracks ahead of the party while others slipped past them to take up positions on their flanks or rear. There was no running away now, and dozens of cloudy, red wolf eyes were trained directly at the party.

"Talk to them, Sonja," said Hennet.

"I don't need to," Sonja replied. "I know exactly what they'd say. They want us to come with them."

To prove the point, the wolves behind them took a step forward.

"A wolf escort," mused Regdar. "I sure hope they take us someplace good."

At that, they all started moving. At the first navigable ravine, the wolves directed them upward, climbing to the top of the hills. The wolves directed them vaguely to the northeast. "At least they're taking us in the right direction," Lidda quipped as the wolves led them farther into the cold zone.

For hours they proceeded through the snow-covered hills and valleys, an unceasing march. Whenever one of them slowed or threatened to stop altogether, a quiet growl, a threatening glance, or a slight nip kept them moving. Occasionally more wolves joined the pack, silently appearing out of the gloom and taking their place among the lupine escorts. Some of them were black, some were white or brown, some old, and others little more than pups. Some were pristine and clean while others' muzzles were coated with blood.

On the whole, the party was probably traveling at a better pace than they would have if left to themselves, as the wolves leading the way broke a path through the deep snow, easing everyone else's passage. Moreover, they proceeded in what Sonja believed was almost exactly the same direction that she'd been headed, but the exertion of the march left them cold, dispirited, and ill-prepared for combat. Sonja tried using her magic to communicate with the wolves, but she could not get a more telling statement than, "Don't resist."

"Why are we doing this?" Hennet asked under his breath, even though he didn't expect the wolves knew what he was saying. "I think we still could fight off these wolves, especially if I dropped a fireball right in the middle of them."

"I don't like being out of control," agreed Regdar. "Perhaps we should try something bold."

"Make one threatening move and you'll be torn to shreds," promised Sonja. "We've killed enough wolves today. These animals are under the control of something unnatural. I want to know what." She paused before adding, "I want to free them."

Eventually they left the hills behind and entered a new landscape. It was mostly flat, though still with occasional rises and cliffs, and under their feet there was the vague impression of sponginess, as of a frozen moss floor. All around them the land was dotted with small, snow-covered mounds.

"What are these, Sonja?" asked Lidda.

"Trees," the druid said, "or what's left of them. This is the

Fell Forest. Remember when the gnoll said that its home was destroyed by the weather changes? I didn't think it meant that quite so literally. Nature has been dealt a cruel blow indeed."

When they passed close to one of these mounds, Regdar, moving slowly enough to not alarm the wolves, scraped some ice off its top. Underneath was the jagged impression of a tree stump. Everything that previously was above the stump had been torn away by a mighty force.

"Well, what happened to the trees, then?" asked Hennet. "I don't see them anywhere." The wind at this moment was reasonably strong but not so forceful that it could tear a tree in half and deposit it miles away.

Sonja looked up at the sky. It was a menacing mixture of gray, white, and black. "The weather in this zone isn't predictable. Those winds last night were fierce, but they were mild compared to whatever did this. Maybe they deposited the trees far from here. Or maybe somewhere up there—" she pointed at the white sky— "those tree trunks are still flying away, waiting for the winds to let up, waiting to drop."

"Yondalla protect us!" swore Lidda, casting a nervous glance at the sky. "I don't want to be standing underneath them when they do."

"No," agreed Regdar. "Nor do I want to be here when those winds start up again."

The wolves quickly moved the party to an area clear of the stumps.

"This must have been a convenient path when the forest was still here," said Sonja. "The wolves keep to the habits of their forest home, even though it's now destroyed." She felt sorry for them, though she knew that these highly adaptable creature were far better suited to this new landscape than most animals.

This clinched one thing in her mind, at least. These

wolves, or most of them, were native to this area. The snow-bloom she'd found was certainly not, and she'd seen ample evidence of a strange influx of new life in the cold zone. But an influx from where? How could a fully grown snowbloom appear in a place that wasn't even snowy two weeks before?

"Sonja," complained Lidda, "how much longer can they lead us like this? My legs feel like they're going to fall off."

"It can't be much longer," Sonja said.

One of the wolves stopped, its ears perked straight up and its head twisting to the right, looking off into the snow. One by one the others followed suit, bringing the pack to a solid halt. A shape appeared out of the snow, a large form lumbering on all fours. Its fur was stark white, darkened only by a black nose dotting a snarling muzzle. Approaching the wolves, it rose onto two legs before letting out a deafening roar.

This cannot be, Sonja thought. A polar bear! Here? So far from open water, so far from the arctic? She wanted to think it had escaped from some degenerate carnival or from some rich man's private menagerie, but she knew the truth. It did not belong here. It was an interloper, a herald of the new landscape, ready now to do war with the vestiges of the old.

The wolves answered the charge, rushing forward to confront this new enemy, leaping, snarling, biting at its exposed flesh. The bear swung its frost-covered claws, crushing skulls and cracking ribs wherever it found a target. The limp corpses of wolves slammed back against oncoming attackers. The bulk of the wolves circled the bear to get onto its exposed flanks or to try a leap onto its back. The bear shifted its weight to crush the wolves, but they still came, biting, scratching, ripping at the bear wherever they could. The bear roared with pain but was undaunted, even as the wolves tore huge chunks of flesh from its sides. Blood flowed through the snow in red streams. In confronting this new enemy, the wolves seemed to have forgotten the four prisoners.

"What do we do?" Hennet whispered to Sonja.

"We can escape," said Lidda, but Sonja still stared at the violent spectacle, wondering whether to intervene.

Regdar stepped up behind her and placed a hand on her shoulder. "Sonja," he said, "do you remember what you said when Hennet wanted to attack that dragon? You said our mission was to find the origin of the cold zone and stop it. Everything else is secondary. I think that once we find and stop the source of this ice, all of our other problems will fall into line, including these wolves. This is our chance to escape without hurting any more wolves. This chance might not come again. We should go."

Regdar's wisdom caught her by surprise. After a moment's hesitation, Sonja turned away from the wolves and the bear. The wolves were slowly wearing down the bear, clinging to its back, forcing it down onto all fours.

"Quickly then," Regdar whispered. They had barely set off when a loud howl sounded from behind them. They turned and saw something else appearing from out of the swirling snow. It was white, just like the polar bear, but it was no bear. It looked like a huge wolf, so enormous it towered even over the polar bear, but its size made it impossible for this creature to be a wolf. It was like nothing they'd ever seen. The snow swirled around it, as if trying to avoid landing on this beast. Its sharp, blue eyes glinted with a wicked intelligence.

The great wolf reared back, lowering its head parallel to the rest of its body so it pointed directly at the bear. It opened its mouth as if to growl, but something else entirely came out instead. A high-pitched shriek sounded, then a few blue-white streamers crept out of its maw toward the bear, followed a few seconds later by a brilliant ice-white cone that burst from between its open jaws. The cone expanded outward, catching the bear and all the wolves that hadn't scrambled away. The bear tried to roar, but no sound came out. Caught in the wolf's breath, its flesh froze within seconds. The wounded bear died quickly, but the great wolf kept exhaling its frigid breath, harder and longer, until the bear was no longer flesh and blood but something as fragile as ice.

Moments after the giant wolf stopped its onslaught, the bear's neck snapped under its own weight. The head fell off and rolled some distance before coming to rest.

The humans and halfling stood still, unsure whether to run or fight. The great wolf turned its blue eyes to them and with a single leap landed before them with such force that snow flew into their eyes. The surviving wolves, many of them battered and bloodied, ran to join it, forming a circle around the prisoners once again. The polar bear had killed many wolves, but enough remained to form a solid ring.

"What is that?" whispered Lidda.

Sonja knew exactly what it was and met its piercing glare.

"This is a winter wolf," she explained to the others. "My parents and I faced them on occasion. We killed them any time we could. They're cruel, wily creatures that operate as scouts for the frost giants. They're powerful and evil. They serve no useful purpose in nature."

"They're intelligent?" asked Regdar. "Could it behind all this?"

"I don't know," said Sonja. "It's possible but not likely."

"What do we do?" asked Hennet.

"Leave it to me," the druid answered, clutching her cudgel tightly.

The winter wolf bared its teeth as it ambled leisurely to the party. When it opened its mouth, it was not to freeze them with a breath but to speak. Its wolfish lips moved as a human's might, and it spoke in distorted Common!

"What have my children brought me now?" it said, its voice a distant growl rising in its throat.

"These are not your children!" cried Sonja. Then she

snarled back at it as a wolf might, barking and growling. The other three stared at her, astonished. Of all the things they'd seen this day, this was the strangest yet.

"Let us keep to human language," the wolf said in its own tongue. "Otherwise it would be unfair to your friends."

"No," replied Sonja. "I can translate for them if I must. Your pack must hear what I have to say."

"Impertinence!" the wolf snarled. "I am the First Son of the Cold, the Archhunter of the Frozen Drifts of Daak. I am Savanak! I shall rip your friends to shreds to feed my pack and chew your slender form to whet my own hunger!"

"You shall not!" Sonja barked back. "I am a Daughter of the Endless Glacier! I have faced your kind before, Savanak! I have slaughtered them and removed their hearts for trophies!"

"I know of no Endless Glacier," the wolf countered, "and I know of no human who can make the claims you have."

"I challenge you, Savanak," Sonja said. "I challenge you for this pack, for leadership of all the wolves under your command. I make this challenge against your honor according to the ancient rules of wolf-kind, laws far older than man. You must obey. To deny such a challenge is an admission of cowardice."

The winter wolf switched to Common. "You cannot make this challenge!" it growled. "You are not a wolf."

"Neither are you," the druid spat back. She tossed her cudgel to the ground. Staring down the winter wolf, she lifted her arms so that a strange, shimmering light overtook her. Before the eyes of her companions her form warped. Her face distended, her nose slid forward, and her robes changed from white to gray and from gray to black, the material sprouting thick fur. Her hands shrank and grew claws, and a slender tail sprouted from her back. She slid down onto all fours, fully transformed into a tall, jet-black wolf.

The emotions felt by the other members of the party ranged from amazement to shock to fear. No one, not even Hennet, had ever seen her do this before. They all knew, of course, that some druids were capable of making such transformations, but they didn't know that Sonja could.

Anxious to assuage their fears, Sonja approached her companions. They instinctively pulled back, but she kept her tail low, her face open and docile. She approached Hennet and rubbed her furry cheek against his leg. Hennet cautiously ran his hand over her head, tousling her ears and feeling the contours of her doglike skull. Her hair was soft and silky and her eyes, now shaped like a wolf's, were still Sonja's soft blue. Some ineffable essence of Sonja shone through them still.

"Foolish hound!" Savanak roared. "Do you think your cheap magic trick impresses me?"

Sonja, now capable only of wolf language, snarled back.

"This is no trick. I command the forces of nature, the same forces that hate you and that you despise. My challenge stands." She cast a glance at Savanak's wolf minions, standing attentively on the sidelines. "They accept it, so you must as well."

"You are beneath me, runt human." He spat out the last word with particular venom.

"Prove it," said Sonja. "Do it without your breath weapon."

"And you without your degenerate spells."

"So let it be," said Sonja, "for the leadership of your pack. Your pack may not intervene—"

"Neither may yours." Savanak pointed with his muzzle at Regdar, Hennet, and Lidda.

Unable to speak Common in this form, she turned to the others and pointed as a bird dog might to an area farther away. The wolves ringed this exposed area, marking off something like a crude arena.

"I think she's telling us to back off," said Lidda. "She wants to fight this creature alone."

Regdar protested vehemently. "Sonja, don't do this! It's almost twice your size. Fighting together, as a group, we can beat this monster. You don't have to do it alone."

The wolf that was Sonja shook her head and turned her back on them. Reluctantly they slipped back. The wolves parted to let them through and closed the line behind them. Several wolves broke ranks and settled into the snow next to them, silently and calmly staring at them, almost daring them to interfere with this battle over honor.

Sonja stalked the makeshift arena, eyeing her larger adversary. "If you should violate our agreements," she reminded the winter wolf, "know that you risk bringing your pack down on your head."

"Quiet yourself and fight," said Savanak. He lunged at her with all his weight. The wolf was fast but not as maneuverable as the smaller Sonja, who nimbly dodged the attack and raced off to await the next assault. She hoped she could tire

Savanak enough to gain an advantage, but it was a risky endeavor. She was tired from the long march with the wolves, and even now she was beginning to pant. Fortunately she knew enough about the winter wolves of the Endless Glacier to improvise tactics.

Winter wolves were usually barding natural pack animals, individually powerful but usually banding against more powerful foes. The few remaining mammoths still wandering the icy tundra were hunted mercilessly by winter wolves, less for food than for the challenge of bringing down the largest animal of the far north. Soon, Sonja knew, there would be none left, and humans wouldn't be to blame. Fortunately, this winter wolf was on its own, and they were less adept at fighting alone.

Growling softly, the winter wolf kept its ground. Its otherworldly, blue eyes glowed in the cold, taunting her from across the snowy arena. It bared its teeth ever so slightly, and froth started to spill from its mouth.

"Keep the lines around us," said Sonja, casting a sidelong glance at the wolves surrounding their arena, and Savanak snarled in agreement. She charged straight toward Savanak but swerved to the right at the last second, giving the winter wolf tempting access to her undefended flank. The wolf took the bait, snapping at her as she passed. Sonja was faster and evaded his jaws and used the opportunity to make her own attack. She jumped against Savanak's white flank and slashed her claws into his flesh. Her teeth cut into the wolf's back. But the larger wolf whirled, shaking her off before her fangs could cause real damage. Sonja swiftly withdrew to the sidelines. Dark, red blood trickled down Savanak's white fur. He twisted back his head in frustration. The wound was placed just so that Savanak couldn't lick it.

Sonja had drawn first blood, and she could hear Lidda's excited cry, but Sonja was disappointed. She'd hoped to bite the wolf's spine, paralyzing it and ending the match quickly. Savanak was now wounded, angry and twice as dangerous. Saliva dripped from his pointed teeth. Sonja snarled at him from the sidelines, luring him forward, praying Savanak would commit a reckless act.

She hadn't lied when she said she'd killed winter wolves. Her parents waged guerilla wars against them on the stark tundra, separating them from their packs and slaying them without mercy. The young Sonja occasionally participated in these campaigns, and once or twice she was even allowed to make the death blow. But to tackle a winter wolf in battle alone? Her parents were stronger druids than Sonja was now, and a winter wolf was a difficult kill to make even for them.

Savanak thrust forward toward Sonja, tearing up the snowy ground as he went. He anticipated Sonja's dodge and met her with all his weight. But he hit an icy patch and his speed was so great that even the sure-footed beast of the tundra could not stop himself. Sonja lowered herself to the ground to snap at the tall wolf's legs as he skidded past, hoping to sever a tendon or cripple a joint. Instead, Savanak's massive paw caught her hard in the face. Sonja tumbled away, and the winter wolf plowed through the pack members lining the sides.

"Keep the lines," Sonja barked to the surrounding wolves.

The winter wolf bounded back into the arena and the ring closed again.

All the while, Sonja planned. If she couldn't best the wolf in strength, she thought, she must find another way. She knew winter wolves were hotheaded. Perhaps she could drive him to a reckless rage. A blow made in anger might be a careless blow. Sonja and Savanak kept to opposite ends of the arena, staring at each other across the snow, waiting for the other to charge.

She taunted Savanak in his own language: "What troubles you, Savanak? Can the mighty wolf not defeat the runt human? You are not a fit ruler for this wolf pack. The winter wolves of the Endless Glacier were mighty, noble foes. You are a short-furred lapdog next to them!"

"Human bitch!" Savanak roared. "I could shatter your skull with my jaws."

"Step forward and prove it!"

Sonja raced toward the middle of the arena, and Savanak sprang forward to meet her. The winter wolf swatted at her with its huge paw and caught the side of her neck. She landed on all fours and sprang again, but Savanak was ready for her. He caught the ruff of her neck in his teeth and bit into the loose flesh. The powerful creature swung his head, throwing Sonja, who seemed no heavier now than a child's doll, through the air. She landed hard in a splatter of blood.

Lidda shrieked from behind the ring of wolves, but Sonja barely heard it.

The wolf approached her slowly, not cautiously but brazenly, lording its power over her. Sonja turned her head to face it, and from her supine position she gave a defiant snarl. Savanak took a slow, deliberate step forward, jaws positioned to snap her neck. He closed in and Sonja could feel his frigid breath.

At the last second, Sonja pulled away and sprang into air, sailing clear over Savanak. Drawing on her last reserves of strength, she became a whirlwind of fur and teeth. She kicked up large amounts of snow until one entire side of the cleared space was lost in a white cloud.

Savanak reared and scanned for her through the haze. Even the enhanced senses of a winter wolf could not find her now.

"Do you think you can hide from me?" he asked with a soft growl before plunging headfirst into the snow. But he could not gauge the other side properly, and once again he disturbed the lines of the arena. Crouching in the settling snow, Sonja was reassured by the growls of warning that drove Savanak back into the arena. The pack would enforce the terms of the challenge. Alone, perhaps she could not defeat this winter wolf, but with help . . .

The cloud of snow she had kicked up was nearly gone. Sonja leaped out at Savanak, catching his flank with her claws and tearing a red line down his ribs. When Savanak turned to snap at her, she was gone again, taunting him from the far side of the arena. When he rushed toward her, she used her speed and maneuverability to hop away to the opposite side.

Both wolves were wounded and trailing blood across the snow when they leaped at each other. Both were tired and weakened. Anger rose in Savanak. Sonja could see the change in his eyes when she stared at him from across the arena. Again they traded sides, but the druid refused to get close enough to attack or be attacked. She was no longer trying to end the challenge at all but to drag it out.

"Craven human!" Savanak growled. "Fight me! Fight or yield." Sonja didn't return the taunts or respond in any way. She stared at him from across the arena.

Savanak's blood boiled. The winter wolf howled shrilly to the heavens. Summoning his energy, he sprang forward at Sonja with all the speed he could muster, teeth snapping, blue eyes flaming. Sonja pushed off the ground and only barely sailed clear of Savanak's mighty jaws before the juggernaut stumbled through the wolves forming the arena's outer lines.

One bold wolf, offended by Savanak's repeated violation of the confines of the challenge, offered a warning by nipping the winter wolf on his rump. This proved a bad idea. Savanak reared back instantly and crushed the wolf's skull with a clamp of his mighty jaws. Outraged at the needless slaying, another wolf jumped in for Savanak's throat, but the winter wolf struck it in the chin with a paw. The force of that blow snapped the wolf's neck and flung the body backward into the pack. Other wolves stood their ground, jaws open, backs raised in anger, but Savanak ignored them. He turned his attention back to Sonja, who stood at the center of the arena, a lupine approximation of a smile crossing her snout.

"The lines must not be disturbed, Savanak," she reminded him.

Rage blinded the winter wolf and all reason left him. He reared back, mouth opened wide. A high-pitched sound emanated from Savanak's mouth, and a few cold, blue streamers began issuing forth. Instantly, the wolves on the sidelines broke ranks and rushed forward at their leader. The winter wolf's attack was cut short by a dozen wolves' slashing jaws tearing at his flesh. Savanak howled as they bore him down, tearing chunks of meat from his flanks and snapping at his neck to make the kill.

Sonja issued a single, sharp bark and all of the wolves stopped where they stood. Limp and bloodied herself, she struggled to her feet, then slowly transformed back to her human form.

Hennet, Regdar, and Lidda rushed to her side. She was bruised and cut, and she limped, but the glow of victory shone from her.

"You won, Sonja!" Lidda shouted. "You're the pack leader now!"

Hennet closed his arms around Sonja. She stiffened slightly as he touched a delicate spot.

"Thank all the gods you survived," he said. "I thought I'd never see you again."

"How did it work?" asked Regdar. "Just because the winter wolf was about to use its breath?"

"That was a clear violation of our conditions," Sonja explained. "It didn't hurt that Savanak kept breaking the enclosing lines, too. I won by default. Not the most glorious way to win a challenge, but it did work."

"You taunted your opponent into violating the rules," Lidda said, "and that disqualified him, or it, or whatever. In halfling society there's no more noble victory."

Sonja smiled at that thought. "Let's see what's left of Savanak." She gestured for the wolves to back off her opponent then picked up her cudgel from where she'd dropped it earlier. The winter wolf was a bloody mass. His belly still heaved, but he was completely incapacitated. Savanak would soon bleed to death, Sonja knew. She could only guess whether a winter wolf in such a state would answer questions truthfully, but it was worth a try.

"You traitorous runt!" the winter wolf swore at her in Common. "You won through deceit. Allow me the dignity of death."

"Not yet, Savanak," Sonja answered. "You are bested and, yes, you are dying, but you will answer my questions. How did you get here?"

"I don't know," the wolf spat. "A magical force ushered me here while I slept. I considered it a blessing from the gods. The Frozen Drifts of Daak were far behind me, a new pack followed me, and no others of my kind were near to compete with. Bliss." Savanak's upper lip curled high above his teeth.

"What destroyed this forest?"

"It was stumps when I got here. The wolves said the first blast of this cold took the trees but left them. It is strange magic."

Sonja eyed Savanak suspiciously. "Where did you arrive?" she asked.

"At the core—the center of the area, or so I took it to be. It's the coldest there, and there the towers of ice reach to the sky."

"Towers of ice?" asked Sonja.

"The dragon keeps its lair there," the wolf explained. "The white. I saw it when I arrived. It stared at me like it wanted to fight, but then it flew away. I wandered through the forest of stumps until I found this pack, killed its leader, and made it my own."

"What has caused all this?" demanded Sonja. "Where is the ice coming from? How can it be undone?"

"I don't know, druid bitch!" the wolf snarled. Its voice was fading. "The wolves tell me that a few humans passed through the forest some days before the ice began. Perhaps it was they who did it. Go to the towers of ice if you feel the need. Fouler things than wolves lurk there. I hope they rip the frozen flesh from your bones!"

The ice druid gestured with her cudgel, inviting the wolves to finish off their fallen leader. They rushed forward and tore into the shaggy body ferociously, swalling hunks of meat as the winter wolf howled his last.

Sonja turned to the others. "The towers of ice—that must be the zone's center. We might still reach there today if we hurry. We must get moving."

"You can't travel like this," Hennet said, wiping away blood from her.

"Don't worry," said Sonja. "I can heal myself more swiftly than I can heal anyone else. I'm not even that badly hurt. I made it look worse than it was for Savanak's benefit."

"What about your new friends?" asked Lidda, gesturing toward the gruesome spectacle of the pack devouring the winter wolf.

Sonja made a wolfish bark, and all the wolves turned their attention back to her. She uttered a few more noises until they lowered their heads in reverence and returned to their meal.

"What did you do?" asked Regdar.

"I relieved them of my rulership. It's up to them to select a new leader by ordinary wolf means. They'll trouble us no more."

"I'm glad to hear that," said Lidda. She looked around at the forest of frozen stumps stretching in every direction. "Do we even know in which direction these towers of ice lie?"

Sonja pointed. "This way. The wolves say so. I'd ask them for an escort but . . ."

"I think we're doing just fine on our own," said Regdar.

"I'd agree with Regdar," said Hennet, adding, for once. "I've had quite enough of wolves for one day."

"Have you?" laughed Sonja, smiling to bear her teeth.

"I didn't know you could do that when we first met," said Hennet. "I might have been a little more careful with what I said."

"It's not just her, you know," Lidda told him. "Every woman is a wolf."

The farther they traveled toward the core, the colder it became. They weren't there yet, but Hennet could not imagine anything being much colder than he was. Pelor's sun barely shone in the sky through the impenetrable clouds. The snow was up to his knees. He wrapped a fur around his face and looked out from behind it only to keep himself from walking into one of the stumps and falling face down in the snow. Sonja knew several spells that could increase their resistance to the elements, but the magic's duration was short.

Walking indefatigably into the wind, her white face bared to the onrushing cold, blonde hair whipping round her head, Sonja didn't look like any human being so much as a snow sprite or some other, otherworldly creature born of ice.

Soon they discovered a cave at the base of a cliff which was reasonably sheltered from the weather, and they decided to rest there a while. In this place they discovered a used torch that seemed fairly new; it left a black line of charcoal when Lidda ran it against the cave wall. It must have been left by the other party of humans who crossed through this area slightly before the plague of ice began and whom Savanak had mentioned, they decided. Was that group responsible for all this? The cave itself seemed too perfect to be a natural formation. The walls were smooth and rounded, suggesting a magical origin.

They couldn't stay long in this shelter. Sonja wanted to reach the "towers of ice" before dark, so after healing wounds and recovering spells, they set out into the snow again.

Regdar carried Lidda on his broad shoulders. Hennet considered offering to do this himself but realized that his slender shoulders were far less appropriate for Lidda than Regdar's. The snow on the ground was too deep to be traversed by her short legs. Regdar matched Sonja's pace, and Lidda leaned over to ask her something.

"Sonja, do you get cold?"

"I'm cold right now," she explained. "I'm not immune to low temperature, but I generally don't mind the cold. Take me to some tropical beach and the story might be entirely different."

"So being an ice druid . . ."

Sonja finished Lidda's sentence. ". . . grants me considerable resistance to the cold, yes, but not immunity. When I was growing up, cold was neither bad nor good, it was just how things were. Cold is not uncomfortable for me, at least not generally."

"So you've never really felt cold?" asked the halfling.

"Once," said Sonja.

"When was that?" asked Lidda.

She was interrupted as the druid started suddenly, surprised by something overhead. All eyes turned to the sky where, barely visible amid a torrent of snow, a thin, white form was passing almost directly over them, just at the limit of their vision. Its color was more like enamel than snow and glistened in the light. Its wings were streaked with light veins of blue and purple. Their span somewhat greater than its length, which was scarcely the height of a human, and they were flapping furiously in the heavy crosswind. The sound of that flapping was the thing Sonja noticed. If the dragon was aware of the party, it showed no signs.

The druid whirled to face Hennet in time to see him launch a magic missile directly at the dragon. The bolt zipped to its target and blew a small hole in one leathery wing. The beast let out a high-pitched, reptilian squeal and turned to face its attackers. It spotted the party instantly then pointed its nose down and launched a sharp dive directly for them.

Sonja, Lidda, and Regdar fumbled for their weapons as Hennet readied another spell. For a moment he contemplated using the wand of fire, but Sonja had cautioned him to preserve that if at all possible. A white mass of sticky fibers flew from his hands toward the dragon. This spell was usually used at close quarters to entrap and incapacitate, but Hennet was trying a new application for it. The web exploded in front of the dragon to trail fibrous strands across its face and body. Suddenly unable to flap its wings or even see, the beast plunged downward. At the last moment it tore through webs and spread its wings, pulling out of its dive just feet above the ground. As it whistled past Hennet and the others, the speed of its passage kicked up a thick cloud of swirling snow.

They stared into the wall of snow, ready for the dragon to burst out and launch its icy breath against the party. A shriek sounded from the cloud, but no dragon appeared, only the end of its tail which for a moment snaked free of the wall before pulling back. For a full minute they waited, watching the cloud of snow filter out.

Hennet stared at the empty field ahead of them, puzzled. "I scared off a dragon?" he asked in disbelief. "I scared off a dragon with a web spell?"

"You shouldn't have attacked it at all," growled Regdar. "Remember what Sonja said before? On the wing, it could have killed us with ease."

"Hey," shot back Hennet, "I saw a monster, and I reacted. Let's not forget that I was the only one who thought quickly enough to save us back there."

"You wouldn't have needed to if you hadn't put our lives in danger to begin with," protested Regdar.

"I think we're missing the larger issue here," said Lidda, still perched on Regdar's shoulders, which were now heaving with anger. "Why didn't the dragon attack us? It looked pretty angry to me."

"Perhaps it saw a family resemblance," Regdar muttered.

Lidda ignored him. "Something made it retreat, and we should figure out what. Sonja?"

The druid's brow furrowed. "It may have been acting on orders."

"Orders not to kill us?" asked Hennet.

"Maybe just orders not to let itself get distracted," Sonja explained. "The most important question would be, who's giving the orders?"

"Frost giants?" asked Regdar. "Are we talking about frost giants?"

"By all the gods, I pray not," said Sonja. "My parents very rarely fought frost giants directly. They're fifteen feet tall and have legs like tree trunks. With the combined powers of us four, we might be able to defeat one of them. But," she added, "they very rarely travel alone."

Sonja's words left the party demoralized. Hennet took it on himself to put things right. "Remember why we became adventurers and not merchants or tanners or cobblers. We all had a choice. Let's remember why we chose this."

Lidda smiled slightly, and even Regdar was inexplicably cheered by Hennet's insight.

"So let's get moving," the sorcerer said. "These towers of ice can't be very far now. The gods know it cannot get much colder than this."

Lidda rested on Regdar's shoulders as they plunged through the snow, covering her eyes to protect them from a barrage of hard snowflakes. She considered this undignified, the kind of thing humans did with toddlers, but it was necessary for the moment. She recalled an old fable that her grandmother once told her. It concerned a young halfling named Burrowling. Burrowling feared the cold more than anything in the world. When winter rolled around, he'd lock himself in his room and refuse to come out until the spring thaw. He barricaded himself in with supplies enough to last the season and never even poked out his head to see what was going on. He was utterly convinced that the cold would be his death. Burrowling missed out on playing with his friends, going to school, learning his trade. In the summer he was a friend to everyone, but in the winter he never set foot outside of his home.

One year, Burrowling met a beautiful female halfling named Endra, whose skin was white as snow. They fell in love. But as he felt the days growing shorter and the wind growing colder, Burrowling realized he didn't want to spend another winter locked in his room, so far away from her. Knowing that Endra would never agree to spend the winter in his room, he suggested they leave the village and go south to a place where it was never winter. Endra agreed, and they set off.

Burrowling gave up everything he ever knew when the two of them went south together. They walked through human and dwarf lands where halflings were regarded with amusement or slim tolerance, and they continued on. Ultimately they came to a sunny land called Calandra where the locals swore that winter never came. There they settled down. Burrowling built a house for Endra and hoped they would be happy for all time.

When the first day of winter came, it was as balmy and warm and sunny a day as Burrowling ever knew. Endra asked him for the first time why he was so scared of the cold. Burrowling admitted that he didn't know, which made Endra weep.

"Why are you crying, Endra?" asked Burrowling. "Is it because you are so far away from your home and your family?"

"No," Endra said. She put her hand against Burrowling's cheek. It was cold as ice.

"I am the cold," Endra explained. "I took halfling form to wander the world, and I fell in love with you, the halfling who fears me more than all things. Why? Why do you fear me so much?"

Burrowling cried, and his tears froze. He clutched Endra's cold form in an embrace, and together the two of them transformed into solid ice. Their house changed into ice, and the ice spread over all the land. No longer the hottest of lands, Calandra felt its first winter, and its cold lingered ever since. The frozen forms of Burrowling and Endra, fused together for all time, stand there still.

As a child, Lidda had been greatly puzzled by the story of Burrowling and Endra. Perhaps its meaning was that people shouldn't be afraid of the cold, but the image of Burrowling and Endra transformed into ice made Lidda fear the cold more. Many years had passed since she'd thought about it, but now it came back to her. Probably it meant nothing and was only a tale to entertain listeners. She wondered if she should share it with the others.

They heard a heavy, stomping noise in the distance. It was a series of hard clomps, one after another, emerging loudly from the snowy gloom. The haze was so thick they could hardly see in front of them, and the reverberations caused the snow to tremble all round them.

"Our dragon?" asked Hennet, "back for more?"

"No," said Sonja. "It's something on the ground. It sounds a little like a mammoth, but something that large couldn't pass easily through these stumps."

"So what could it be?" asked Lidda.

"Shh . . ." said Sonja. "It's coming closer. Get ready."

Regdar swiftly strung his longbow and readied an arrow. On his shoulders, Lidda did the same with her crossbow, while Hennet prepared to launch an arsenal of magic at whatever might appear from the white veil in front of them.

When it did arrive, the image was so nightmarish and unexpected that all of them hesitated. Even Sonja stared openmouthed at this new threat. A great scorpion was approaching them from the snowy gloom.

Lidda was the first to react as the monster scuttled forward. She fired her quarrel. It struck the frost-encrusted scorpion on one of its pincers but bounced off harmlessly, barely having made a mark. Regdar's arrow struck harder and embedded itself in one of the creature's legs but didn't slow it at all. Hennet launched a spread of magic missiles, but these, too, had no apparent effect on the advancing monstrosity.

As it drew closer, they could see that this was not a giant scorpion coated in frost. Rather it was actually composed of solid ice.

"What do we do?" Hennet asked Sonja. She shook her head.

"I have a suggestion," said the sorcerer. He pulled the wand from Atupal off his back. "Fire should do the trick."

"Everyone get back!" the druid shouted.

They needed no more urging to speed away from the giant ice monster. Regdar clutched Lidda's ankles with one hand, pinning them around his neck to keep her from being jounced off his shoulders. Looking back over her shoulder, Lidda saw that their foe nearly matched their pace. Its eight legs carried it above the tangled stumps at surprising speed.

Hennet also risked a look back. "Shall I do it now, or are we too close?"

Sonja shook her head. "We need more distance."

But they didn't seem to be increasing the distance. The scorpion showed no evidence of falling behind, and in fact it seemed to be gaining on them.

Looking back at this image of frozen fear, Lidda observed that it didn't walk like a normal scorpion, small or large. The scorpions she'd seen generally kept their bodies close to the ground with their legs arched above. The stumps that littered the ground made that impossible here. Instead, this beast raised itself on its spindly legs to lift above the obstructions. She could see its belly, and that made her think . . . even a creature made of solid ice probably was more vulnerable on its underbelly than anywhere else.

"You want it slowed down?" Lidda asked. "Watch this."

Swiftly she stood on Regdar's shoulders and sprang backward to land feet-first. The snow reached up almost to her neck, but she used this to her advantage. She dropped to her knees and burrowed below the surface of the snow to conceal her exact location from the icy behemoth. She felt the cold intensify as the monster approached. When one of its legs speared through the snow beside her, she sprang forward and plunged headfirst under the icy body.

For all its terror, the scorpion was a thing of beauty when seen up close, like an intricate, gorgeous ice sculpture come to life. Every leg, tail section, and pincer looked as if it were carved from a single block of impossibly pure ice. Lidda could see right through the thing. The sight was distorted but unobstructed by any visible organs that might be vulnerable to attack.

She drew her sword and thrust upward with all the force she could manage. The blade penetrated the ice with a shower of chips, and Lidda pushed it in hilt-deep. No blood flowed, and the scorpion never made a sound, but it reacted in obvious pain, shuffling backward and trying to dislodge Lidda and the sword. The halfling held onto her weapon with all her might. She heard the clack of Regdar's arrows striking the scorpion. She watched Hennet's magic missiles strike the scorpion's midsection. The ice refracted the image so that it looked to Lidda like a kaleidoscopic comet exploding into a carnival of light above her.

The scorpion tried to smash its body downward to crush Lidda, but the stumps beneath it prevented its weight from falling on her. Frustrated, it chased after the others but paused to lunge downward again any time it entered an area with fewer stumps. Lidda knew that it was only a matter of time before it found an area sufficiently bare to flatten itself, and her, against the frozen ground. She yanked on the sword but couldn't free it, so she let go and slipped into the snow. Moments later, the creature maneuvered over a clear spot and flopped down, but all it succeeded in doing was driving Lidda's sword even farther into its insides.

Lidda raced through the snow, plowing through drifts almost as tall as herself. She climbed atop one of the broken trees and leaped from stump to stump while waving furiously to the others. In its preoccupation with her, the scorpion had fallen behind the others, giving Hennet the room he needed to launch his fireball, if Lidda could get clear. Her short legs were no match for the nimble ice monster's, though. Even with her sword driven into it, the scorpion was able to keep up with her. Part of her wished Hennet would just broil the damned thing and let her take her chances.

Regdar's arrows and Hennet's spells did little to deter the monster's relentless pursuit.

"We have to stop it!" shouted Sonja. "It will catch Lidda and kill her!"

The druid looked at Hennet, standing at the ready with his wand of fire, wordlessly asking her for permission. She shook her head—there was too much risk of Lidda being caught in the blast. Sonja considered trying to draw a lightning bolt down from the storm, but she rejected the idea for the same reason. Her control over the spell was too coarse. She would only put them all at greater risk.

A cold smile crossed her face briefly. "Save that fireball," she called to Hennet before sprinting away from the others and toward the unearthly monster.

"What's she doing?" asked Regdar.

Hennet shrugged. He had long since stopped asking that question. He was just happy that she seemed to have some plan.

As Sonja ran, she extended her hands in preparation for a spell. When she thrust them forward, the scorpion burst into blue fire. The brilliant, azure flames shimmered across its icy back.

"What?" Regdar stammered. "How can ice burn?"

Hennet laughed, understanding instantly what Sonja had done. "She's clever! It's not real fire but faerie fire. No heat, no smoke, just light. Pray that the monster doesn't know the difference."

The giant scorpion had never seen fire before, let alone

been engulfed by it. As a creature of ice, however, its fear was instinctive. Too wide and bulky to roll over, it spun instead, desperate for some way to tip itself onto its back. Lidda was forgotten. Sonja rushed back to join the others, and Hennet lifted the wand, readying it to launch the fireball.

Lidda tried not to look back to see what Sonja had done, but when she heard the sound, something between a campfire crackling and a lion's roar, her curiosity won over. She spun on the top of a stump just long enough to see a blood-red sphere of flame rocket across the field from Hennet's wand. It struck the ice scorpion with thunderous force. The explosion sent a wave of flame roaring out in all direction, incinerating stumps, evaporating snow, and scorching the frozen ground. She felt a blast of heat against her face. The warmth was jarring. When the flames flickered out, the scorpion was reduced to a puddle of hissing slush.

Relieved, Lidda waded back to the others, avoiding the scorched area. She could hear Hennet's exclamations of glee long before she reached the sorceror.

"That was beautiful," he shouted. "It worked perfectly!" His arms were wrapped around Sonja. "That thing didn't know what hit it!"

"What was it?" asked Regdar. "That's what I'd like to know."

Lidda congratulated Hennet with a sincere "Well done."

"Many thanks." He bent down and clutched the halfling by the waist before lifting her up to his eye level. "What about you?" he gushed. "Diving under a giant scorpion with nothing but a short sword? If that's not heroism, I don't know what is." He kissed her on both cheeks before plunking her back onto the ground.

"Unfortunately," continued Hennet, "that's it for the wand of fireballs. When they gave it to me in Atupal, they told me it had only one more blast in it. I hoped they might be wrong, but they weren't. That's it for the big fireworks. " He tossed the spent wand aside.

"My sword!" Lidda said, looking back at the scorpion's molten corpse. "Do you think it survived?"

"Maybe," said Hennet. "We should look for it before that melted mess can freeze solid again."

Hennet and Lidda's jubilation faded when they saw the concerned expression on Sonja's face. Regdar stepped up next to her, looking every bit as stern. "We can celebrate later, you two," he said. "We need to know what that was, and we need to know if there are any more. Sonja?"

"Whether there are any more I can't say," the druid said. "Nor am I entirely sure what it was. I've certainly never seen anything like that on the Endless Glacier. But I've heard stories. . . ."

"What kind of stories?" asked Lidda. She wondered if there might be some connection to Burrowling and Endra.

"I've heard that many creatures native to this plane have equivalents, like them in most ways but wrought of solid ice, living elsewhere."

" 'Elsewhere'?" Hennet asked. "You mean, as in other planes?"

"Cosmology is not my specialty," Sonja said. "Like all of you, I'm sure, I've heard of the elemental planes. There are planes of fire, water, air, and earth, each of them populated by elementals and other creatures of those elements. On the borders of those planes are other, smaller, and less-known regions where the elements mix. Perched between the planes of water and air is the quasi-elemental Plane of Ice."

Regdar looked both perplexed and disturbed by Sonja's conjecture. "You think that creature was native to the Plane of Ice?"

She shrugged. "I can't be sure, but that would be my guess. If someone or something opened a portal to the Plane of Ice, that could be the source of the scorpion, the winter wolf, and all this ice and snow. That doesn't explain everything. It doesn't explain how a fully grown snowbloom turned up in an area that wasn't even cold a few days ago, but at least it's a theory, which is more than we've had so far."

"Sonja," said Hennet, "aren't you jumping to conclusions? Maybe that ice scorpion was created in some evil mage or priest's laboratory. Isn't that possible? We don't even know for sure that this Plane of Ice exists."

"I know," said Sonja. "It exists. I've been there."

Stunned silence fell over the others. "When? How?" asked Lidda.

"All of those wishing to be druids must pass through some sort of extreme test of endurance. Many initiates die, and the ritual is seldom spoken of. My test was to spend time on the Plane of Ice. My parents opened the portal for me."

Sonja looked at Lidda. "You asked me before if I was ever cold, and I said I was once. This was the time." She closed her eyes as if trying to block out an unpleasant vision. "I don't know if I can describe it to you. There's no sun, no moon or stars. There's no natural heat from any source. Fires won't burn. The wind never ceases howling. Blizzards last years, icebergs are the size of continents. The cold there is simply unimaginable.

"I was there for only a day. When my parents retrieved me I was frozen nearly to death. I have seen the Plane of Ice, my friends, and I have no desire to see it again."

Hennet's exhilaration over defeating the ice scorpion was soundly demolished. "What happens if we don't seal the portal?" he asked.

Sonja answered, "Our plane eventually becomes like the Plane of Ice."

"Then we must not fail," Regdar said with utter conviction. He lifted Lidda onto his shoulders. "C'mon, Lidda. Let's go find your sword." They left Sonja and Hennet alone.

"Don't be so crestfallen, Hennet," Sonja said. "Remember why you became an adventurer."

"I always try to," replied the sorcerer. "Still, at moments like this, I wish some other adventurer were doing this instead of me."

"Hennet," she asked, "do you love me?"

Hennet was taken aback at the question. Instead of answering, he simply stared.

"It doesn't matter," said Sonja. "It doesn't matter if you love me or if you don't or if you're envious of Regdar or he's envious of you. It doesn't even matter if I love nature and despise civilization. In the face of this, none of our concerns matter. The worst things we dared to dream are all true, and it's up to us to set it right."

"That's very humbling, Sonja," said Hennet.

"Is it?" she said softly. "I think rather the opposite is true. The heroes on whose stories you were weaned had no personalities, no personal concerns. They were not people, and neither must we be. If you want to be a hero of legend, the hero who saves not just the girl, but also the world, this is your chance. But if you become a legend, you'll no longer be Hennet."

There was no mistaking the towers of ice of which Savanak spoke. They were stark, ivory-white ziggurats, reaching so high above the ground that the party wondered why no one had seen them while the Fell Forest still stood. Perhaps nobody ever cared to get close enough to look. They loomed in the distance like mysterious giants—frost giants, of course—standing, watching, ever silent. There were seven of them in all, each cylindrical and twice as thick as any redwood, placed irregularly and unpredictably across a strangely terraced surface where snow collected on different planes. The impression was of a nightmare painting or the surreal contours of a frozen level of the Hells.

"Be on guard," said Sonja as they drew near. "From what Savanak said, this is the dragon's lair. Even if it's not, there's something strange about this." She paused a moment, giving the others a chance to test their skills of observation.

"I think I know," said Lidda. She held up her hand, her palm open against the wind. "Where we're standing," she explained, "the wind is blowing directly at us, from the direction of the towers. But look over there." She pointed to the side. "Watch the snow. It's not going in the same direction at all. It seems to be blowing directly away from these towers, too."

"That's it," said Sonja. "Unless I miss my guess, that means that our portal is someplace in the center."

"Great!" said Hennet. "Now let's get in there and seal it before our dragon friend pays us a third visit."

"Something feels wrong," Sonja confessed as they approached the closest tower. "No guards. Nothing defending the portal. And what are these towers?"

When they reached the closest one, sheltered from the wind behind it, Regdar ran a gloved hand and scraped off the white coating of ice. Underneath, it was smooth and pitch black.

"It looks like basalt," ventured Lidda. "This is really some tower."

Regdar and Hennet brushed off more of the ice as Sonja turned to regard the strange terraces among the towers.

"You see what this is?" she said. "It's a city. Or maybe something smaller, like a military outpost." She took a few steps. Her footsteps showed evidence of stone, not ground, beneath the ice. With a gesture, she cast a spell and removed a large area of ice, revealing a solid gray surface beneath, a perfectly flat and featureless granite walkway. It was not made of slabs laid through manual labor but created whole, apparently through wizardry.

"Mages," she concluded. "Many mages must have lived here."

Hennet concurred. "Who else would live in so many towers?"

Sonja took another step forward, then gave a shriek of surprise. "What is it?" asked Hennet.

"Come over here," she said. The others joined her and instantly understood what she was reacting to. Past a certain spot, the wind stopped. Or rather the wind ceased to exist—

it just wasn't present. Like the eye of the hurricane, this was the calm at the center of this whole magical ice storm. To the party, badly windburned and tired of being pelted with snow and ice over the past few days, this came as a considerable relief.

"We really are at the core," said Regdar. "Then the portal—"

"No one move," blurted Sonja. "The portal could be invisible. You could walk right into it and pass through to another plane by accident."

Sonja closed her eyes for a moment and cast another spell, one that would reveal the auras of magic around them. As she did, some of the party's clothes and weapons lit up with a serene, blue glow, but that was barely noticed amid the blue light that streaked over the entire field. The color that denoted the presence of magic was so strong there that it shone all across the frozen city, draping the whole place in azure tones that flickered and glimmered. Even the faces of the party were painted blue now. The source of this magic was what looked like a large, vertical slit in the air near the center of the frozen city, as tall as Regdar. It was a tear in space out of which energy coursed and flowed, pulsing and seething as it gushed magic.

"So that's what a portal looks like?" Lidda asked. "I've often wondered."

"We not actually seeing the portal," Sonja explained, "but the magic it generates. That's what we're looking at. Seeing it, I now realize it's not a true portal but rather a rift."

"What's the difference," said Regdar.

"A portal is like a door," Sonja explained, "something calculated and measured that was designed to be somewhere. A rift is more like a break or a hole in a wall, a crude, makeshift rip between the worlds. It comes about through violence, not planning."

"Does that mean that it's accidental?" asked Regdar.

"No," explained Sonja, "not necessarily accidental . . . maybe just crude. If you can't find a door and you really need to get across, you might just a tear a hole in the wall."

Regdar nodded.

"Unless I miss my guess . . ." Sonja led them around the rift, keeping a cautious distance from it until she reached the opposite side. From there, it couldn't be seen. Only a vague, blue emanation of magic remained.

"It's gone!" said Lidda.

"This is difficult to understand," Sonja explained. "As I said, I don't know that much about cosmology." She bent over and made a snowball and tossed it through the rift from behind. It landed with a plop on the far side, as if nothing whatsoever obstructed it. "It only faces one direction," the druid explained.

"Why is there no wind here?" asked Hennet. "I mean, we're right on top of it, so shouldn't the wind be stronger?"

Sonja made another snowball and flung it up into the air. It flew straight up about fifteen feet, but never came down. At that height it was caught and scattered by a ferocious wind blowing outward.

"This is a kind of safe area," Sonja said. "It was probably designed this way to allow the rift to be crossed easily. If this rift was meant for an army to march through, for instance, it wouldn't pay to have them blown away the instant they stepped through."

"You mean," asked Lidda, "that we could step into that . . . and step out in the Plane of Ice?" She was intrigued by the thought.

"If it's all the same, Lidda," said Sonja, "I'd rather dispel it instead. You'll have to satisfy your curiosity some other time, but I strongly advise against it."

If all went well, their mission would end here and now. Sonja stepped forward, staring intensely at the rift between worlds. She raised her right hand, where she wore the silver ring of dispelling given her in Atupal and silently activated it. For what felt like an eternity she peered into the blue, shimmering oval, waging silent war on the rift, the force of her mind and magic against its unfeeling, guileless power.

Doubt wormed its way into her spirit. This rift fought back. She felt it powerfully at the center of the effect, and she still felt it, weaker but definite, at the edges when she shifted tacks and tried to fold the opening in on itself. Every time Sonja's magic pushed forward, the rift's magic pushed back.

Everyone's attention was focused so intently on Sonja and her efforts that no one noticed a white form scuttling down one of the towers, descending the smooth surface with ease. Partway down it launched itself off and cut its way through the snowy sky, gliding in a graceful arc toward the intruders despite the buffeting wind. The blue light emanating from the rift struck the dragon's pearly scales and dabbed them in deep shades of turquoise.

As it closed in, the dragon opened its elongated jaw and let out a shriek. Instantly Lidda, Hennet, and Regdar covered their ears. Sonja, however, was locked in concentration and barely heard the screech. Regdar grabbed her by the arm and yanked, shattering her carefully laid spell. She didn't make a sound or protest but merely collapsed where she stood. Regdar lifted her in his strong arms and ran across the terraced surface of the strange, frozen city.

The hole in the little dragon's wing was still visible, and sticky threads, remnants of Hennet's web spell, still dangled across its face. As if it recognized its tormentor, the dragon swooped directly at Hennet. The sorcerer was caught in an outstretched claw and lifted several feet off the ground before being tossed against the frosted side of a tower. Hennet slid to the ground, moaning and grasping his head, and the dragon managed a reptilian approximation of a laugh as it swooped away.

A crossbow quarrel struck the dragon's tail, penetrating its hide just deeply enough to draw blood. The creature reared about to find the source in time for another bolt to plunge directly into its gaping mouth. A flick of the pale, forked tongue dislodged the bolt, and the head swiveled to point toward a snowbank where Lidda crouched beneath the snow. She thought herself hidden and she might have been to human eyes, but one could not fool a white dragon by hiding under snow. The dragon turned in her direction while letting out a low growl that resonated off the frozen towers.

As the dragon wheeled above the towers, the duration of Sonja's spell ended. The blue aura indicating magic vanished, taking any sign of the rift along with it, but it was still there, still invisibly pumping more and more snow onto this plane. It was easy enough to recognize where it was even without magic; it was the spot above which all the winds originated and away from which all the snow streaked.

Regdar, meanwhile, dashed about trying to find a safe spot for Sonja, who was still unconscious in his arms. Part of him wanted to set her on the ground, draw his greatsword, and plunge into the fray, but he could not abandon the druid. He watched helplessly as the dragon swooped toward Lidda's position, until Hennet launched a magic missile that caught the dragon from behind. The beast swooped high up into the air this time, training its attentions on the scampering Hennet. Lidda fired another quarrel from her crossbow, but the dragon was too far above and the bolt, carried away by the crosswind, never reached it.

While other dragons breathed weapons of fire, lightning, or gas, a white dragon's breath was a sustained funnel of ice. It was said to be more cold than any natural chill. Hennet wondered how much colder anything could be than what he'd already felt in the last days, but with the dragon hovering above him preparing to launch its breath weapon, he wasn't anxious to find out. Aching and bleeding, he pulled himself to his feet along the side of the tower and crawled along its circumference to the far side, facing what had been the forest. He hoped to keep the tower between the dragon and himself, but the creature caught onto his plan quickly. It alighted vertically on the side of the tower. With its wings folded in, it scurried sideways down the glazed walled with perfect grace, rushing toward Hennet, moving to bring him into the range of its breath.

At this moment Hennet wished he hadn't used up the only charge on the wand of fire. The dragon's ability to scale walls was probably limited to those covered with ice, so even if a fireball didn't kill it, a good blast of heat might still send it crashing to the ground. The wand was out, but the thought still gave Hennet an idea. He jogged away to put a bit of distance between the tower and himself, but did not flee. Instead, he fired a magic missile upward, not at the dragon itself but immediately in its path, against the white surface of the tower.

When the missile struck, it exposed a huge, black patch of the basalt surface in the dragon's path. This barely slowed the dragon as it heedlessly crawled its way past, but a split second later, the impact of the spell set off a chain reaction across the tower. Portions of the ice coating the tower slid free, including the portion beneath the dragon's claws. Unable to cling to cling to the sheer surface, the dragon tried to spring into the air but couldn't manage to get off the slick basalt surface. Its outstretched wings sought the air, but too late. Headfirst, it plunged toward the icy ground.

This time Hennet ran not as a lure but for his life. He slid around to the opposite side of the tower and ran back toward the center of the tower cluster, in the direction of Lidda and Regdar. He heard a thundering crash behind him but didn't turn back to look.

Lidda watched as the dragon thrashed on the ground, trying to untangle itself. Moments later, it swooped out of a cloud of snow and flew almost at ground level after Hennet. She readied her crossbow but then heard a strange noise from above her shoulder. It sounded much like a voice—a flinty, high-pitched, child's voice.

"Don't worreee about him," it seemed to say, giving a strange trill to the r's. "Watch."

The dragon bore down on Hennet, teeth snapping and talons clutching forward. Just as it was about to snatch him, a dark hole opened at Hennet's feet, and he was gone.

Above the wheeling, screeching dragon, emblazoned on the side of the tower where the ice had peeled away, stood the emblem of Wee Jas, rigid overlord of death and magic.

Regdar watched from around a corner, with Sonja still limp in his arms. She felt warm and soft, but he had little time to reflect on this. He blinked, trying to figure out where Hennet had gone. It had happened so quickly. Had he fallen into a hole in the ground? That was the best Regdar could figure, short of teleportation magic.

Cheated of its prize, the dragon snarled and circled back and landed to search the spot where Hennet disappeared. Its muzzle snuffled over the snow, trying to uncover a secret door. As long as it kept this up, Regdar thought, the rest of them were safe.

Then Regdar, too, heard a strange voice, accompanied by a fast buzz like the sound of a hummingbird's wings.

"Look to the leffft," it said. "Look to the tower."

Regdar looked for the source of the voice but couldn't find it. He did what it said and saw that a door stood open on one of the towers a short distance away. The dark hole beckoned him.

"Get to safety. Quickly!" the voice instructed him.

Regdar looked to Lidda and saw that she, too, was looking toward the open door. When their eyes met, they shared a look of puzzlement and concern, but their options were few.

The dragon shifted its attention from Hennet's mysterious disappearance to the others. It spotted Lidda first and flew toward her. She scrambled for the open door.

"Hey!" Regdar shouted at the dragon. "Over here!"

The beast turned to face Regdar, then he, too, bolted toward the door. Sonja was light but Regdar felt her weight keenly as he pushed his legs to their fastest, kicking up clouds of snow as he ran. Regdar could hear the smooth beats of the dragon's wings behind him, drawing nearer and nearer.

Lidda was almost at the door. Regdar was sure she'd be safe, assuming that safety actually lay through that door, but he couldn't say the same for Sonja and himself. He thought he could even feel the dragon's chill breath on the back of its neck. It seemed so close and the door so far away. Part of him wanted to turn back and confront the dragon, but he knew he couldn't put Sonja down or draw his greatsword before the dragon would be on him. He ran on, and the cold along his neck was gone and the doorway yawned before him. Either he had outrun the dragon, or it had given up for some other reason. He raced through the dark opening just behind Lidda, and the door slammed behind them.

They were shut in the dark. For the first time in quite a while, they had real shelter. In fact, it was just as cold amid these ancient walls.

"What just happened?" asked Sonja, who slid groggily out

of Regdar's arms. She leaned against a wall to steady herself.

"We'll tell you when we figure it out," said Lidda.

"The dragon attacked us," said Regdar. "There was an open door on one of these towers, so we ran inside. I heard a voice telling me to do it."

"So did I," Lidda said. "I didn't know what else to do, so it seemed like a good suggestion at the moment."

"And Hennet?" Sonja sounded desperate. "Where is Hennet?"

"Down below." The voice was the same one both Lidda and Regdar had heard before. They jumped, shocked to realize they weren't alone in the dark. Regdar's hand went to the hilt of his sword, but Sonja put her hand over his.

"What are you?" the druid asked. "Can we see you?"

"I have a light heeeere. Don't be afraid. No fire! No fire!"

A magical torch set in a knot on the wall flared into light. Lidda, Regdar, and Sonja found themselves staring into the leering, red face of a great horned creature, its mouth wide open revealing dozens of white teeth. For an instant they thought this mouth was doing the talking, but it was an intricate carving set into the slate-gray wall of the chamber. Its long, thin arms ended in jagged claws, and a set of spines ran along its back and onto the tail that encircled the entire room, where a thin, circular stairway snaked up and down the tower.

The creature depicted in the carving was a tarrasque, the most fearsome monster of legend, but another, very real monster was in the room as well. Crouched on the floor was a thin, ethereal being that was only slightly taller than Lidda. It certainly wasn't any halfling. Its skin was the chill blue of a frozen ocean, and two leathery wings were folded behind it. Two tiny horns topped its hairless head. Its nose was large and angled, and saurian ridges traced along its icy limbs.

Lidda was shocked by the demonic appearance of this being. Was it some sort of imp or quasit, she wondered?

Sonja knew better. "You're an ice mephit," she said.

"Yeess," it answered, giving the vowel a proud trill, "a mephit." And it offered a little bow.

"A mephit," said Regdar. "What on earth is a mephit?"

"A creature born of the elemental ice," explained Sonja. "Like an elemental, only more concrete in form." She turned to the little creature. "You're from the Plane of Ice, are you not?"

The mephit nodded. "The othersssss come with your friend." The mephit's wings suddenly unfurled behind its shoulders but never flapped as it levitated a few feet off the ground. It rose to eye level with Sonja and studied her face intently. "Yoooou are warm and yet you are cold. You are not like the others."

Sonja didn't appear uncomfortable talking to this bizarre creature hovering inches from her face.

"I am a druid of ice," she told it. "I used to encounter your kind on the Endless Glacier where I grew up."

The mephit cocked its head in unfamiliarity. "Endless . . . Glacier? I know it not."

"I'm not surprised," Sonja said. "You're no longer on the Plane of Ice."

The creature grumbled to itself. "Thiiiis we know. The great winds blew us through the hole in the planes. We are stuck now. You must help us."

Regdar and Lidda didn't know what to say as they observed this exchange.

"Sonja," Regdar said, eyeing the mephit suspiciously, "are these creatures evil?"

"Neither evil nor good, in my experience," Sonja said, some annoyance apparent in her voice at being asked such a question in the creature's presence. "They did not aid the frost giants, nor my parents. They lived alone in secret and made alliances with no creature." She turned her attention back to the mephit. "Now you want us to help you?"

"Times are strange," the mephit said. It hovered back to the ground and let out a piercing squeal. Somewhere down in the dark, another squeal echoed.

"Your friend is below with the otherrssss," the little creature said. "We must go down." It unfolded a single wing to indicate the stairway leading down. "There all we will explain."

"What do we do, Sonja?" asked Lidda.

"That's easy," said the druid, removing the magical, smokeless, heatless torch from the wall. "We go down."

She took a step or two down then hesitated as she peered into the blackness. Her knees felt suddenly weak, and she almost dropped the torch. Regdar grasped her arm in support, but she shook him off. She knew she needed to be strong and to lead, no matter how unsettled she was in these close quarters.

The others followed Sonja down the stairway, which wound straight down some twenty feet before stopping at an archway. The opening led to a vast, open area beneath the frozen city. Slender pillars supported the ceiling, and massive, circular walls marked the locations of the towers above, like great roots extending into the earth.

"Yondalla above," said Lidda as she looked around the room. "Whoever built this place didn't do anything small, did they?"

The incredible depiction of a tarrasque was nothing compared to the mural that lined the outside of the cylinder from which they emerged. Beasts of legend frolicked in gardens and infernal flames. Griffins floated through the heavens and serpents stalked the oceanic depths. Titans battled fiends, heroes confronted dragons, and set between them were arcane glyphs and writings in ancient languages. No vault any of them had seen contained such art, nor any king's palace. The walls of their cylinder were only the beginning. Along the floor and the other cylinders they could see similar images, all coated with a layer of clear ice that clung thickly to the walls and distorted the images through its ripples.

The ice had taken its toll down here, too. The floors were slick and frozen, and portions had warped and heaved up under the cold. Huge icicles hung precariously from the roof like the stalactites of a cave, threatening to fall at any moment. The magical, white torchlight struck the ice and sent strange reflections all along the walls and floor, and a tiny army of reflections followed along as they walked.

The occasional decayed desk or bare table stood next to the cylinders, some of them collapsed and broken. The mall looked unused for centuries. The impression was of a vast storehouse, fairground, museum, dance hall, or dining hall, an all-purpose subterranean meeting ground for the wizards who lived in the long-neglected towers above. To Sonja, Regdar, and Lidda, this place seemed like a blow to the heart, not only for its size and intricacy but also its emptiness. It felt every inch as desolate as the snowy, white world through which they'd just come.

This wasn't an expanse of nature, free of man. It was a relic of man's faded glory. It was a tomb.

Their mephit escort had little patience for the newcomers'

awed stares. It let out another high-pitched squeal, and another replied from across the cavernous hall from the dark. The sound grew in echoes until it had the force of a jungle cat's roar.

"Your friend should be in that direction," the mephit explained. As they crossed the marble floor, keeping their footing carefully on the slick ice, their every footfall echoed throughout the hall.

Hennet was easy to find. He was backed against one of the cylinders, using his short spear to hold at bay a whole colony of ice mephits. There were about a dozen of the creatures. All of them looked almost exactly like the first, with only small deviations of size and face to tell them apart. The art on the cylinder depicted a stark starfield. Hennet and the mephits seemed to be floating together in a void. With the torch brought close, Hennet could finally get a good look at the things surrounding him.

"Hennet!" Sonja shouted. "Is that any way to greet our hosts?" Her voice reverberated throughout the mall.

The sorcerer turned to face Sonja. At that moment four or five of the mephits leaped into the air, swiftly grasping the shaft of his spear and ripping it from his hands. These mephits flew off with it while the others surrounded Hennet, hovering mere inches from his face, as if daring him to make any move. The mephit who greeted Sonja, Regdar, and Lidda flew over to join them and was soon indistinguishable from the rest.

"Please!" yelled Sonja. "We have an opportunity here. Let's not spoil it!"

"He killed three of ours already," whined one of the mephits. "We saaaaved him, and he repays with death!"

Lidda and Regdar looked up to see a small trapdoor built into the ceiling. A feeling like a small tremor spread across the room, and the trapdoor shuddered above them. Somewhere off in the darkness, an icicle was shaken lose by the vibrations and crashed to the floor.

"They attacked me!" protested Hennet.

"Only because he attacked usss first!" another mephit shouted.

"Please, please everyone," Sonja said, lowering the pitch of her voice in hopes that cooler heads might still prevail. "We're together in this thing. We must cooperate if we're to accomplish anything. I ask you to release Hennet, and Hennet, you must be calm. Just come over here."

"He is dangerous!" shouted another mephit. "A killer! You ask us to free him?"

"I ask you to give him a chance to repent for his mistakes," Sonja said. "He never would have killed you if he knew the truth."

"What truth?" Hennet shouted at Sonja. "What are these things?"

"With any luck," the druid told him, "they're our new friends."

With that, the mephits relented at last, pulling away from Hennet, dropping his short spear at his feet. He cautiously bent over to recover his weapon and walked over to join the others, dragging the spear's point on the floor. They kept a collective scowl trained at him, as if to say that they would have their revenge yet.

Again, the trapdoor above them rocked under a draconic assault.

"You killed some of them?" Sonja whispered into Hennet's ear. "You don't know what you almost did."

She turned her attention to the mephits, crowded around a small corner of the floor, all of their unearthly blue eyes staring at their human guests.

"I am Sonja of the North," she said. "These are Regdar and Lidda. Hennet you've met. We came to this city to investigate the origins of the cold that is currently expanding and devastating the countryside. We encountered the dragon up there several times in the past few days."

Lidda and Regdar exchanged a worried glance behind Sonja's back. Why was Sonja telling these monsters everything? She said they weren't evil, but that didn't make them friends.

"He is called Glaaaze," explained one of the mephits. They seemed to have no obvious leader. A different mephit spoke almost every time.

"Glaze," Sonja asked. "Is he the one who did this? Unleashed all this ice?"

The mephits nodded fervently. One of them proclaimed, "With the Ilskynarawin!"

Sonja shook her head at the difficult word. "The . . . Ilskynarawin?"

"It's an artifaaact," said a mephit. "It tears a hole in the worlds. Brings ice onto Prime. This issss what has happened here. It blew us through, and now we can't go home."

"It does more than that," supplied another. "It summons. It summons creatures of ice here. It turns place into cold place."

All this would explain how Savanak got here, Sonja reasoned. He was probably native to the plane of ice, but a powerful summoning spell uprooted him from his home and placed him here. That would explain the snowbloom, the polar bear, and other oddities of the cold zone. But the mephits' description also set off a long-lost twinge of memory in the back of Sonja's mind, something her parents told her when she was a child.

"The Frozen Pendant," she said. "I think I've heard of it, under the name 'the Frozen Pendant'."

"What do you know?" asked a mephit.

"Only a story I heard as a child," Sonja said. "I always thought that my mother invented it, but maybe not. It took place in an ancient kingdom in the middle of a hot desert. I don't remember many of the details, but there was an evil, foolish chancellor or vizier who presented a piece of jewelry to the sultan. The chancellor opened a box, and when the sultan touched the pendant, it erupted with ice, killing him, the chancellor, and everyone else. The ice went on to devastate the entire kingdom."

"There's a halfling story not unlike that," added Lidda.

"It may or may not have beeeen the Ilskynarawin," a mephit offered, "but 'Frozen Pendant' is a good name."

The others nodded in agreement, their little heads bobbing up and down aggressively.

"Where is this Frozen Pendant now?" Regdar asked.

Every one of the mephits faced the ground. "Down, down, down. Hot down. We cannot go. You may go, not weee."

"Slow down," Sonja said. "Tell us about Glaze. Tell us how all of this happened."

The mephits whispered to each other for a moment in an unintelligible language all their own. Regdar took the opportunity to whisper in Sonja's ear.

"Are you sure this is smart?" he asked the druid. "How can we know they aren't deceiving us?"

"I don't," Sonja confessed, "but they saved our life. We should at least listen."

"The dragon Glaaaze," said one of the mephits suddenly, "lived far to the north, where his kind were being slaughtered by giants of frost."

"That could be the Endless Glacier," said Sonja, "where I was born. How do you know?"

"He told us when we arrived. He wanted us to stay in this new snow world. But we want to go back home."

"Why can't you just walk through the rift again?" asked Regdar.

The mephits talked to each other in their own language,

almost as if they were deciding on the proper response. "Wii-inds!" one shouted. "We get blown back through."

"You refused to cooperate with Glaze?" asked Lidda.

"And he killllled some of us."

"We took refuge in the towers . . ."

". . . where Glaaaaze cannot reach us."

It was unsettling the way the mephits began and ended one another's statements, sometimes switching speakers two or three times per sentence.

"He is young but smart, for one of they, one whiiiite," other mephits said. "He did not want to fight giants. So he left."

"He wanted to find new place, place free of giants."

"He traveled from snow-capped mountain . . ."

". . . to snow-capped mountain. For a while . . ."

". . . he finds peace, but older, more . . ."

". . . aggrrrressive whites live . . ."

". . . there already and force him . . ."

". . . out."

"But he heard about Ilyskynar . . . Frozen Pendant. He heard it here, in lost city in forest near mountains . . ."

". . . he went seeking. Many yeeears he search forests. Find nothing."

"Then he finds this city, in this forrrrrest. He searched city . . ."

". . . breaked through to this underground. Open . . ."

". . . doors to towers, searched towers. Maked lair . . ."

". . . in one tower, broken . . ."

". . . open at top."

The mephit extended a wing to one of the cylinders in the distance, indicating the bottom of one of the great towers. A tremendous pile of broken wood was heaped against the door and welded together with ice, meant to keep the dragon out. Sonja assumed this was the work of the mephits' icy breath—not as strong as that of a white dragon or a winter wolf but still potent.

"And then," a new mephit took the dialogue, "heeee found a stairway . . ."

". . . down, down, down."

"He follow. Into hot place. Hot . . ."

". . . place under towers."

"Magically heated," reasoned Hennet. "Too hot for you to go there yourselves?"

The ice mephits shuddered at the thought. "Boil, sizzle, boil!"

"You mean," said Sonja, "that Glaze found the Frozen Pendant somewhere beneath this underground mall. When he activated it, the rift opened, and you were blown through along with the elemental ice."

The mephits nodded together.

"Earlier," said Lidda, "we encountered a creature that looked like a giant scorpion, only it was made of ice. How did it get here?"

"Wander through rift," several mephits explained. "Probably not only. Door between worlds open. Strange thiiings happen."

"If we manage to restore summer," said Sonja, "such aberrations will die in the sun. Can we undo what Glaze has done if we get the Frozen Pendant?"

"Bring to us," said one of the mephits, and the others joined it in a chorus. "Bring to us! Bring to us! Bring to us!"

"We know what to with iiiit do," one of them assured the party.

"Can't you just tell us what to do with it?" asked Regdar.

The mephits shook their heads in unison, obviously anxious to dispel this idea.

"Too tricky," said one.

"Too dangerous," chimed another.

"Only make things worse," offered a third. "We must do."

"It's still down there?" Sonja asked. "Glaze didn't take it with him?"

"No," said one mephit. "We search."

"Not up here."

"Down there."

"We sure."

This made a certain amount of sense to Sonja. If the artifact was kept in a magically heated area deep below the city, it was possible that Glaze, a creature of the tundra but still more capable of weathering temperature changes than these mephits, would leave the Frozen Pendant below. The most likely creatures to seek it would be those like these mephits, composed of ice itself and therefore unable to venture into a hot area. Whether the young, inexperienced white dragon was intelligent enough to make such a plan was another question entirely.

"So you want us to go down and find the Frozen Pendant for you?" Hennet asked. "What do we get if we do this?"

One of the mephits shrugged oddly. "No more ice!" it shrieked with something vaguely like a laugh. The others joined it, until their shrieks were so loud they were nearly deafening.

"Stop!" shouted Sonja. "That's too much." The mephits stopped, but the distant reverberations continued for many moments.

"This is too much for me as well!" said Regdar. "Let's do as they say."

The mephits led the four newcomers to the cylinder that they explained would lead down to the "hot place" where the Ilskynarawin, the Frozen Pendant, awaited them. Here there was no stairway going up but only a smooth, spiral walkway leading down into the gloom. Regdar held the magical torch, which blanketed the room's smooth walls in an unflickering, white light. The mephits refused to enter the cylinder but instead clustered outside the doorway. Regdar noticed that this cylinder, unlike the first, had a door. With a nod to the mephits, he banged it shut.

The moment the door closed on them, Sonja turned to Hennet. "Did you really have to kill three of them?" she demanded, jutting a finger against his chest. "After they saved your life? Did you think that was appropriate gratitude?"

"It was dark, and I had only moments before been staring into the mouth of a dragon! Not to mention that I had just fallen twenty feet onto very hard ice! I felt something buzzing all around me, I heard those little wings of theirs flapping, and I reacted as any one of us would have. I don't like them, those cold little eyes watching me . . ."

Lidda stepped between them. "It turned out all right. The question now is, can we trust them?"

"Who ever heard of a creature from the planes that wasn't happy to come to the Prime?" asked Regdar.

"That may be true of demons and devils," replied Sonja, "but mephits are neither."

"So you think we should do what they say?" Hennet asked the druid.

" I don't relish the prospect of going down there," she said, casting a fleeting glance at the darkness below them, "but I don't see what choice we have. And they did save our lives. I don't have much experience with mephits, but I know them to be aloof in their dealings with humans. Those mephits were desperate for our help.

"That's one side," she continued. "At the same time, there are elements of their story I have a hard time believing. I doubt a white dragon, especially a young one like Glaze, would have the intelligence to seek out and activate an artifact the way they described."

"But you still think we should do what they say?" said Hennet. "For all we know, they're sending us down there hoping we'll get killed."

"One may lie and still have good intentions. We're not dealing with humans. Mephits may have very different ways from ours. We can't assume they wish us harm."

"We can't assume they wish us well, either," Lidda added.

The druid ignored the remark. She stood tall to make a pronouncement. "Before we go down there, you all know that I'm not very comfortable in confined quarters, particularly underground. Black walls are the worst of all, the most unnatural. You selected me earlier as leader of this party, but I think I won't prove a very good choice for what's coming."

Both Regdar and Hennet began to speak, but Sonja shook

her head. "We should follow Lidda. If it's a treasure chamber we're seeking down there, it will be protected by traps. I'd rather put my trust in a rogue, if it's all the same to you."

Regdar and Hennet both shrugged, but Lidda's red face beamed. "I'll be delighted to lead the way. We small folk often find ourselves overlooked, even among our friends. I'm glad to see that's not the case this time."

With that, she made a graceful pirouette and took the first step down the spiral ramp. The walkway looked far more treacherous than it was, but they proceeded cautiously anyway. Down they marched, taking each step carefully and deliberately, maintaining large spacings between themselves. Their passage was wordless as each wondered whether he or she would climb back up that ramp again.

The ramp spiraled down through many turns. At the bottom, the air felt distinctly warmer than above. It was still cold, but pleasantly so.

"I can see why the mephits couldn't come down here themselves," said Sonja. "Even this meager warmth would be highly uncomfortable to them."

"Fire must really do a number on them," Hennet mused.

A single hallway proceeded to the right, narrow enough that two of them could not walk through it abreast. Lidda took a tentative step into it, carefully eyeing the walls, ceiling, and floor. All were as smooth and black, perfect and featureless as the outsides of the towers but without the intricate artwork they had seen elsewhere. To Lidda, this was another demonstration of the building's magical origin. This was not a place for show. Rather, it was utilitarian and blank. Neither was there any evidence of the vermin, molds, and fungus typical of most ancient, underground passages she had explored.

"I don't suppose any of you valiant spellcasters has anything in the way of a foolproof spell to find traps?" asked the halfling, looking back at the others.

Sonja and Hennet shook their heads and cast each other concerned looks.

"Just as well," said Lidda. "More glory for me. Observe."

She drew her sword and sliced it through the air in front of her. The blade barely completed its arc before an arrow shot from the wall to cross the hallway and bounced off the opposite wall. Lidda picked up the missile and inspected it carefully.

"Barbed tip," she announced then sniffed it. "Not poisoned, though. Anyone fancy adding this to their quiver? Don't worry; if this is the best these dead wizards had to offer, getting through here will be child's play. But take this as a warning—don't step in front of me."

Lidda walked boldly into the hallway. The others followed more cautiously. Regdar noticed that Sonja walked more slowly than anyone and kept her eyes on her feet as she took deliberate steps. It pained Regdar to watch this woman with such natural grace lose her bearings so completely when she stepped out of nature. He decided to distract her with a few questions.

"You said you encountered mephits on the Endless Glacier? What were they like?"

"What?" the druid stammered. "Oh. My parents and I came across a small group of them living near a frost giant community called Jotaralund. We were spying on the giants to see if they intended pushing their frontier to the west, into the Snowswept Flats, which would have endangered the few mammoths still living in that region. Instead of giants bent on conquest, we found a colony of ice mephits, living unseen right under the giants' noses. We invited them to help us in our struggle against the giants, but they refused. They weren't interested in politics, even those that impacted on their lives, nor did they care particularly about protecting nature. They're insular creatures, but not innately hostile to outsiders. They shared with us their observations of the frost giants and let us proceed unmolested."

"So you never had to fight them?"

"No, said Sonja. "Hennet is the only one of us who's done that. They're magical creatures, and they have certain inborn powers. Ice mephits aren't the only kind, you know—there are mephits for all the elements and probably the para-elements too. From what my parents said, all mephits have the ability to summon other mepthits to their side, but there's no guarantee they'll be of the same kind. Ice mephits rarely call for such aid, for obvious reasons. If a fire mephit or a steam mephit arrived, it would scarcely be able to survive in the ice mephit's cold environment, and the ice mephit could be seriously injured or even killed by the blast of heat that would accompany the new arrival.

"They also use their breath as a weapon, like a winter wolf or a white dragon, but it's less potent. And they wield magic."

"What sort of magic?" asked Hennet.

Sonja shook her head. "I'm not entirely sure. My understanding is that they don't cast spells like you or I, but they can draw on innate abilities that have similar effects. Something like your magic missiles but probably not as fierce. You're lucky they didn't use this on you up above. I'm not sure why they didn't, but I suspect it's something they can do only a few times a day.

She paused, then continued. "There's something else, too. Regdar, you may be concerned about this. It shouldn't worry the rest of us too much."

"Why just me?" asked Regdar.

"Because you wear metal armor. They can chill any kind of metal until it's extremely cold—your sword, your breastplate, anything metal. If it's on you, it will become unbearable to touch, and you won't be able to fight well, if at all. The effect fades before too long, but if a fight should break out with the mephits, be ready to shed your armor at the first sign of danger. Otherwise, you could end up frozen and unable to fight.

"Don't underestimate these creatures," she concluded. "They may be small, but that doesn't mean they're insignificant or easy to kill."

"Amen to that," added Lidda, who was smaller still. Then she froze in her tracks, keenly eyeing the floor and walls ahead of her. "There's another trap here."

All three of them behind Lidda likewise stopped, barely daring to breathe heavily.

"Good work spotting it," Regdar offered. "Can you make it safe?"

"I don't need to," Lidda replied. "That's what concerns me. It's already been disabled."

"What do you mean?" asked Hennet, striding up next to her.

Lidda pointed out a thin, horizontal line etched into the wall. None of the others would have noticed it without Lidda's pointing finger to guide their eyes.

"There's a scything blade in there," she explained. "Walk through the hallway without first tapping on this part of the wall and the blade flies out to slice you in two at the waist—or takes your head off, if you're me."

"Delightful," said Regdar, who'd witnessed the effectiveness of such diabolical devices more than he cared to dwell on. "But you say somebody disabled it? Good of them."

"What's more, I don't think it was done long ago," Lidda said, running her finger along the inside of the thin groove.

"Why not?" asked Sonja.

Lidda pulled back her finger. It was covered with a dark brown, powdery substance. No one needed to be told what it was, but Lidda said it anyway. "Dried blood."

"Could it be Glaze's?" asked Hennet. "The mephits said he was down here."

"It could be," Sonja allowed, "but maybe not. Savanak talked about other humans who were heading here just before the cold began spreading."

"Maybe," said Lidda, "but if others came here before us, why didn't the mephits mention them?"

"Perhaps they don't know about them," offered Regdar. "Maybe the mephits hadn't been blown through the portal yet at that time."

"Or maybe," Hennet sneered, "our chilly, little friends didn't want to tell us that we're the second group of fools to tackle this job, because the first group never came back."

"With no other evidence, it's pointless to conjecture," Sonja replied.

"Then consider this," Hennet continued. "One of them—whatever 'them' was—met his fate right here. The question foremost in my mind is, what happened to the body?"

No one answered because Lidda was already proceeding farther along the hallway. Sonja did her best to hold her head high and look straight ahead. The jet black walls that reflected nothing felt closer around her with each step.

Regdar put a hand on her shoulder. Hennet, oblivious to the familiar contact, walked farther ahead, just behind Lidda. He had no intention of getting either ahead of her or too far behind her.

"Does something about this place bother you?" Hennet whispered to the halfling.

"A great many things," she replied. "Do you have something specific in mind?"

"This tunnel is clearly not natural. No tools carved out this hallway—they would have left marks of some kind, even small ones. Magic dug this passage. The dimensions are perfect and the material is perfectly smooth. And yet—"

Lidda finished his sentence for him. "Yet the two traps we've encountered were simple, mechanical machines. You'd think that wizards who could build a place like this would install magical traps, or at least better mundane ones."

"Traps that a thief . . . pardon me, a rogue such as yourself would have a harder time spotting."

"Isn't it curious?" asked Lidda. "It's almost as if those traps were deliberately made simple. Why? Maybe to lure us into a false sense of security before . . . *thwap!*"

Sonja bit her lip and grew even more pale, much to Regdar's concern.

"Please, you two," demanded Regdar. "Some consideration for Sonja."

The sorcerer and the halfling turned back to see the fighter, his hand still on the ice druid's shoulder. She shook and trembled, and tears welled up in the corners of her eyes. Hennet raced back to her.

"Sonja, I'm sorry, so sorry. Look," he said, "maybe you should go back to the surface and keep an eye on the mephits. We'll bring back the Frozen Pendant."

"No," Sonja answered. "I will not go up there and wait for you, like some war widow. I'm just a little . . . out of my element down here, but I can deal with it. Bear with me."

Hennet shot Regdar a stern look, as if to say "I'll take it from here." Regdar automatically retracted his hand from Sonja's shoulder, just as the sorcerer folded her into an embrace.

The warrior gave them a long, hard look, his mouth sinking into a deep scowl, before stepping forward to join Lidda. He bent over and whispered to the halfling, "While we smooth over lovers' squabbles, cities freeze." Regdar strode forward, ahead of Lidda into the hallway.

It was just a moment's lapse, and Lidda was ready to caution him, but before she could say anything, Regdar's foot slipped through the floor. He tumbled forward, grasping fruitlessly at the slick wall for some kind of handhold, before vanishing completely. A loud crash sounded from beneath. The floor looked completely intact.

"An illusionary floor!" cried Lidda. She, Hennet, and Sonja all rushed forward to what Lidda estimated was the edge of the trap area. They feared the worst, until they heard a loud stream of profanity emanating from below.

"Regdar!" shouted Sonja. "Are you hurt?"

"No," came Regdar's voice through the false floor. "I'm an idiot, but I'm not hurt. Something cushioned my fall. I don't know what it is . . . there's no light down here."

"I can dispel this illusion," said Sonja, extended her silver ring, but Lidda said, "No need." She shoved her hand through the floor and held it there for about ten seconds. The illusionary floor flickered before them then vanished altogether. The pit it hid covered the full width of the passageway and extended for a fair length, though not so far that they couldn't jump it if they needed to. Hennet held the torch over the pit, revealing an embarrassed Regdar standing in the pit's center about twenty feet below them.

"How in all the Planes did you survive that?" asked Lidda.

"Well," answered Regdar, "I landed on this." He bent over and his face turned white as he looked up to the others. "It's a corpse."

The dead man's neck was broken, undoubtedly in the same fall that Regdar had just survived. The body was otherwise intact—there were no spikes or other diabolical devices at the bottom of the pit.

The pit was not warmed by the magical heat in the hallway above. Frost clung to the black walls, the fortunate result being that the corpse was not badly decomposed and barely stank.

"Another of the other party," said Hennet. "You're quite lucky to be alive, Regdar."

"I don't suppose any of you have rope?" said the fighter.

The three of them each shook their heads to each other.

"Does he?" suggested Sonja.

"Uh . . ." Regdar bent over and gave the corpse a quick search. "I don't think I feel anything like that. He has a few potions or something. We may as well keep those."

"Fine," said Hennet. "Toss them up here."

Regdar pulled three small flasks from the dead adventurer's belt and threw them upward. The sorcerer grabbed them, one after another, and held them up to the torch for closer inspection. When he did, he almost screamed at the revelation.

"Be careful with that stuff! You can't just toss it around like that. You'll kill us all!"

"You're the one who told me to," Regdar protested. "What is it?"

"It's alchemist fire," Hennet explained. "I've never seen it used, but I've heard very impressive stories about it. It's the liquid equivalent of a fireball spell and just as destructive. You throw it, the flask breaks, and the stuff ignites on contact with air. Fools have been known to open a flask of this, not realizing what it was, and destroy buildings along with themselves."

"This is all very fascinating," Regdar noted as Hennet carefully hid the vials in his cloak. "Unfortunately, I'm still down here in the pit. If anyone has any other ideas, I'm listening."

Lidda looked briefly at Hennet and Sonja before fishing reluctantly in her pocket. "I have just the thing," she admitted, a note of sadness clear in her voice. She pulled out a small bottle of greenish liquid.

"Catch this," she said, before tossing it to Regdar in the pit.

"What is it?" Regdar inspected it carefully.

"It's a potion of flight," explained the halfling. "They were selling them at the magic shop in Vasaria. They weren't cheap, but I decided to get one, on a lark. I thought it would be fun to fly, if only for a little while."

"Vasaria?" said Regdar. "That was more than a month ago. Why didn't you mention this?"

"I thought you might think it was silly," said Lidda. "The halfling who wanted to be a bird."

Regdar smiled at the thought. She meant to use it for fun. "You should have told me. I would have bought one, too."

"Flying inside a dungeon may not be the freest feeling ever," Lidda noted, "but at least the potion will be put to good use. Better than what I intended it for. Drink away!"

The fighter uncorked the bottle and downed its thin, nearly tasteless contents. Nothing happened. "Are you sure that magic store didn't rob you?" Regdar asked, looking up at Lidda, who peered back down into the pit.

Regdar's feet lifted off the icy stone floor. "Oh my," he gasped. He was flying! He kicked his legs but that didn't stop his upward rise. Instead it knocked him into a slow, horizonal spin. He tried waving his arms to steady himself, but this only made him bump against the sides of the pit as he rose. He steadied himself in the center and realized that struggling only made it worse, so he allowed himself to float gently back to the level of the hallway.

He dangled up above the pit, extending a hand upward to keep himself from bumping into the ceiling. He smiled at Lidda as he drifted past her.

"What's it like?" the halfling asked.

"Why not find out?" Regdar was getting the hang of maneuvering now, and he swung his body around until his back was to Lidda. She climbed onto his shoulders, then he leveled himself out parallel to the floor. They flew past Sonja and Hennet and back up the hallway they'd just come through, which Regdar knew was safe from traps. The warrior's heavy armor kept him from going very fast, but that was fine. They were barely five feet off the ground, but the thrill remained as the two of them glided through the dungeon with grace and majesty, like a dragon rider on her mighty steed.

"How much longer will this last?" asked Regdar.

"Probably a few more minutes," said Lidda. Noting that Hennet and Sonja were well out of earshot, she went on, "You have to promise me you're not going to do anything like that again. I know you miss Naull and you don't think Hennet is worthy of Sonja. That doesn't matter. You staying alive is what matters."

The fighter began to object, but Lidda silenced him. "You don't have to apologize. Just remember—Naull may have loved you, but other people still care about you. We'd better get back now."

They floated back up to the others just in time for the spell to fade and Regdar to settle slowly to the floor.

"That's impressive," said Hennet with a smile. "I'm going to have to add a flight spell to my repertoire."

Sonja, too, seemed much more at ease after the playful interlude. Nobody felt the need to castigate Regdar for what he'd done.

Having cleared the pit, they found no more traps for a good length down the hallway. This worried Lidda greatly. She understood all too well why the designer of a dungeon like this would do such a thing: to lure looters, or at least looters less canny than she, into a false sense of security.

She was sure of it when the featureless walls were suddenly interrupted by a mural almost as detailed as those adorning the subterranean mall above. It showed a hand clutching an ungainly black lump with a simple chain hanging below it. There was no body with this hand, only part of an arm in an ornately embroidered sleeve. Radiating out from the lump were shimmering waves of frost, which looked so familiar that the artist could only have witnessed this phenomenon firsthand. The waves rippled over a vast, sandy expanse, leaving the image of a frozen desert kingdom dimly recognizable in the back of the image.

Beyond the image, the corridor came to an end. A forbidding, black door filled the wall ahead. The only two choices were to turn back or open the door.

"It seems your mother wasn't making up that story after all," said Lidda, holding a hand over the intricate display but careful not to touch it.

"I guess not," said Sonja. "The Frozen Pendant must rest beyond this door. Can you pick the lock?"

"Oh, probably," said Lidda, looking carefully into the keyhole. "Ancient locks, modern locks, they're pretty much all the same. Isn't it funny? The rest of the dungeon is made of whatever this black substance is—basalt, perhaps?—yet the locks are still made of good old-fashioned iron."

"Just be careful," said Regdar, and Lidda shot him a look as if to say, You don't have to remind me to be careful.

Lidda worked at the lock for a few minutes while the others stood back, half expecting the door to explode or some monster to smash through. As it was, Lidda cracked the lock with no surprises, and the door swung slowly open, revealing a large, empty room. It was much wider than the passageway and with a higher ceiling. In fact, it looked to be a single, large, night-black cube. Another closed door stood opposite the entranceway.

"After you, noble warriors," said Lidda. She gave a little bow and ushered the others through. Regdar and Hennet looked at each other, and the fighter took the lead, stepping cautiously over the threshold into the bizarre room. He sniffed the air.

Regdar's brow furrowed. "Smells sort of like . . . meat?"

"I think you're right. What is this place?" asked Hennet as he stepped through behind him. Lidda helped Sonja through last of all. Hennet scanned the room and found that every wall, ceiling, and floor was composed of the same material and every inch of it was a uniform, jet black—all but a faint discoloration near one of the corners. He stepped over and ran his foot through it, spreading something across the floor. He held the torch down to it.

"It's ash," he said. "Ash, and something else." He poked the toe of his boot against strange bumps and splash marks that seemed almost to be iron, as if something had melted onto the floor then cooled again.

"Why build a room shaped like this?" Sonja asked.

"Wizards built it," answered Regdar. "Even if they were here right now, there'd be no point in asking their motivations."

Lidda went to work on the far door. No sooner had she slipped her lockpick into the lock than a loud noise came from behind her. All four of them turned to look and saw that the door they had just come through had slammed shut, closing them inside the strange room.

"Don't worry," Lidda reassured everyone. "We'll worry about that on the way out." The expression on her face, though, made it clear to Regdar that she wasn't entirely convinced of that herself.

"If there is a way out," muttered Sonja. She was standing in the dead center of the room, intimidated by the unnatural black walls and trembling slightly. A bead of perspiration rolled down her forehead and onto her face. Her eyes watered, and she tried her very best to resist the urge to complain.

"It is hot under this armor," complained Regdar, adjusting his breastplate.

Hennet felt the sweat building in his armpits and dripping down his sides. "It's hot even without armor. Lidda, I hate to annoy an artist while she's working, but is it possible to pick a little faster?" He walked over to the side of the room and put his hand against the wall but yanked it away in shock.

"This room is an oven!"

Lidda looked back at him.

"The walls are growing hotter by the second," the sorcerer said. He reached down to touch the floor. "And the floor too! It'll burn through our boots in no time."

Regdar frantically cast aside his armor, which was growing hotter. He tossed his breastplate onto the floor, where it formed an arched platform. "Your shoes are the thinnest," he told Sonja. "Stand on it." The druid stepped onto the piece of armor but wondered what good it would do.

"I almost have it open!" said Lidda frantically, "but there has to be a way to turn the heat off. Search the walls, search for a hidden panel or something."

"This heat is infernal!" cried Regdar, running his hands along the near-scorching wall, hopping to keep the soles of his boots from burning. How could something so black be so hot? "What I wouldn't give for some ice right now!"

The sickly, dry smell of superheat filled the air. The ashes on the floor smoldered, and the soles of everyone's boots smoked. Regdar skipped back to the door they'd come through only to find that it, too, was locked. He pushed all of his weight against it to try and force it, burning his shoulder in the process, but the door wouldn't give in the slightest.

"Wait," said Sonja, still perched on the breastplate at the room's center. "This must be a magical effect, and that means I can dispel it using this ring."

"How many more charges do you have on that?" asked Regdar.

"I think just one," the druid answered.

"Then save it" the fighter advised. "We'll need it to use on that rift. Save it until there's no other choice."

The halfling's hands worked on the ancient lock, the only

part of the door that wasn't superheated along with the rest of the room. As the locks were made of iron, she reasoned, it wouldn't do to let them melt. There was, however, a definite danger of the lockpick melting inside the lock and ruining their chances of ever getting through. The sweat dripping off her forehead irritated and clouded her eyes, and that didn't make the job any easier.

"I think I've found something," Hennet announced. He pulled out his short spear and ran it against a subtle crack in the wall, forcing open a sliding panel. Inside, two lips were carved into the stone, like a mouth partially open and about to speak. And speak it did.

"*Etos hui vanots*," the stone mouth said, in a high-pitched, chirpy voice, with a flatly cordial tone. Hennet had seen magic mouths like this before.

"*Etos hui vanots*," the magical construct repeated.

It probably wants me to give it a password, the sorcerer thought. "Uh . . ."

"*Nai vanots*," the lips said with the same, emotionless voice. Then the panel slammed shut in front of Hennet.

"Lidda," Hennet said. "I think you should work harder on that lock."

"Thanks for the advice!" Lidda shouted back. "Very helpful!"

Regdar abandoned the walls and rushed to the center of the room to comfort Sonja. The fighter took a gulp of hot air that burned him from the inside. Around the room, smoke rose from their clothes. The wool of their winter cloaks threatened to burst into open flame. Regdar felt a sudden wave of unbearable heat roll up his side from inside his robes. He realized that the water was boiling in his waterskin. It had blown off its top and now was releasing scalding steam against his naked flesh. With a yelp, he yanked it out and tossed it away.

Regdar wrapped his arms around Sonja, who wasn't

weeping or making any noise, though sweat poured from her temples. She stood still, gently trembling in Regdar's strong arms as might a terrified rabbit.

The threatening black walls blazed as Lidda worked at the lock furiously, drawing on previously unknown reservoirs of strength. She felt on the verge of fainting. Hennet danced at the room's edge, trying desperately to pry open the secret panels once again. Regdar watched the pile of ashes in the corner and wondered if that was one of the earlier party and if so, whether that was the fate that awaited them as well— to be dead and beyond resurrection, consigned to ash that would never be scattered by wind or water. Sonja raised her trembling hand, ready to activate the ring of dispel in an effort to save them and in the process perhaps doom the world to eternal winter.

Regdar saw what she was doing and said, "Not yet, Sonja, hold on just a little longer."

The druid wasn't listening. Her eyes were closed in concentration.

"Sonja!" he shouted at the top of his lungs. Getting no response, he grabbed her ring finger and pulled the magical ring off of it. Sonja looked at him, shocked,

"I think I have it," croaked the halfling with a parched throat. "I think . . ."

She cawed in triumph, deftly hopping backward as the black door to safety flew open. With lightning speed everyone jumped through it, Regdar sparing barely a moment to kick his super-heated breastplate through the door into the next room.

When they were through, the door rolled back toward the close position. Hennet thrust his short spear through the diminishing opening, leaving the heavy door open a crack when it came to a rest. Exhausted and gasping, everyone sprawled on the floor, breathing deeply of the blessedly cool air. Sonja magically filled their boiled-dry waterskins with cold water, which they sucked down desperately, saving the last to splash on their faces.

In a few minutes, heat from the adjacent room stopped rolling through the open doorway.

"I've heard of going from the frying pan into the fire," Lidda quipped, pulling herself to her feet, "but I've never done it quite like that."

Finally, feeling recovered, they looked around to see where they were. It was another room like the last, a large cube in form, but this one wasn't empty. It was almost completely filled with supplies of all kinds. Everywhere they looked, something glinted or glimmered in the magical torchlight. Suits of golden and silver armor hung on the walls, glowing magical weapons rested atop carved teak and mahogany cabinets, potions were stacked in cabinets, and pedestals supported devices of strange antiquity and unknown power.

Lidda and Hennet broke into a smile and took a few disbelieving steps forward. This was what every adventurer dreamed of discovering beyond every dungeon door: an unmolested treasure room. This was the find of a lifetime—the treasury of an ancient society, long past caring or seeking revenge, and filled to the brim with loot.

Behind them, Regdar slipped the silver dispel ring from his pocket and handed it back to Sonja. The druid took it wordlessly and slid it back onto her finger.

"We're rich," said Lidda with a disbelieving smile.

"Riches aren't what we're here for," Sonja reminded them. "We're here for the Frozen Pendant."

"And we've found it," said Regdar, pointing to a corner of the room. Amid a fallen suit of armor and a spilled pile of smashed potions lay another adventurer, dead, his corpse covered with a light layer of blue ice. Frozen on his face was a look of stark terror. Clutched in his hands was a delicate, gold necklace, and dangling from that was a lump of black ice that shimmered with unholy magic and radiated a coldness they could feel from across the room.

For perhaps thirty seconds they stood and stared at the frozen body and the artifact clutched in its dead hands.

"He's a rogue," Lidda pointed out, noting the singed lock-pick set at his waist. "He must have picked his way through that room the same as we did."

"The scout always survives the longest," Regdar said, tousling Lidda's hair.

Lidda smiled back at him. "He may have lived the longest, but that still wasn't long enough. Traps got his friends and they got him, too, in the end." The halfling pointed out a small dart protruding from the man's neck. "He must have pulled the Frozen Pendant off that pedestal there," she pointed out an empty one, "and triggered a poison dart trap. So much for him. I wouldn't touch anything in here for the moment. There are almost certainly more traps."

"So the pendant didn't kill him," Hennet noted, wedging the magic torch into a tight space between two crates. "It just iced him over after his death?"

"Apparently," said Lidda. She prodded the corpse with the

edge of her short sword. The weapon broke a layer of ice around the dead man's leg. "Sonja, in that story of yours, all the bad things happened after the Sultan touched the item, right?"

"That's how I remember it," Sonja said. "If the story is to be believed then it would seem it is activated by touch."

"So if it's already been activated, the pendant must be safe to touch now," said Hennet, and he reached for it.

"I wouldn't do that," said Sonja, grasping the sorcerer's arm. "I suspect very strongly that when this rogue picked up the pendant, he activated the rift above us. I don't know what would happen if you touched it now."

"Are you certain anything will happen?" Regdar asked. "The mephits seemed to think it would be safe enough for us to handle it."

"The mephits lied," she stated. "They said that Glaze activated the Ilskynarawin. That clearly didn't happen."

"Dragons aren't known for their lockpicking skills," said Lidda. "Either our dead rogue and his companions led Glaze through, or—"

"Or Glaze was never down here," said Regdar. "Look around you. Does it look like a dragon was in here? Glaze would have torn everything to pieces."

"But why the deception?" asked Hennet. "You're our expert on mephits, Sonja—why did they lie to us?"

"Easy," replied the druid. "They want the Frozen Pendant. I think they can pass back through the rift anytime they choose to do so. They aren't trapped here at all, they've just decided to stay in the hope of finding some way to recover this device. If we handle it and inadvertently make the rift larger, that won't bother them at all. They don't plan to stay here, anyway. Once they have the pendant, they'll disappear back through the rift to the Plane of Ice and leave us behind with our problems. That's how I see it.

"And," she added, "I don't appreciate being used this way."

"I think I understand," said Regdar. "They want the Frozen Pendant. They can't come down here themselves because it's too warm and also because they could never get through all the traps and locked doors. Now that we've cleared the way for them . . ."

"Have we cleared the way?" asked Hennet. "Aren't the locks still intact? That door closed on us all by itself, and so did this one." He pointed to his short spear, still keeping the door open a crack.

"The doors probably lock themselves," Lidda agreed. "It's a magical thing. I've seen it in mages' dungeons before. But who knows how long that takes to work. As it is, the doors, or rather the door, may still be more sensitive to being opened by force."

"I tried to force the far door," said Regdar. "It didn't work."

"But you were forcing it from the inside," Lidda reminded him, "and it opened into the room. It may be easier to force from the other side."

"So what do we do?" asked Hennet, growing increasingly frustrated. "Those little winged bastards lied to us, tricked us into doing their dirty work for them, and we're still thinking of making the delivery for them. I should have killed more than just three of them."

"Hennet," said Sonja, "we don't know what their intentions are. Maybe—"

"Maybe they want to turn our world into an outpost for this Plane of Ice. Sure, they didn't open the rift, but I bet you anything they shed no tears over it. They probably want this amulet to widen the rift, to let more of their friends through. And I'm damned if I'll deliver it to them on a platter!"

"What do you recommend instead?" Regdar demanded of the sorcerer.

"I recommend we take the artifact, we figure out how to use it, and we seal that rift ourselves." Hennet leaned over the corpse, grasped the golden necklace, and pulled it back, shattering the ice lining the man's body. A few fingers snapped as Hennet wrenched the artifact from the dead fist. Sonja muttered a half-hearted protest, but it was no good. Hennet moved toward the light and closely inspected the hunk of black ice that was the Ilskynarawin. To stop its swinging, he cupped it in his hand.

The ice shone brighter for just a moment before erupting with a brilliant flash of light. When this faded away, the piece of ice was the same, every contour identical, but for the color—it was transformed into a brilliant white. Hennet looked on it in awe. He dropped the cold lump of ice from his palm, leaving the necklace dangling around his fingers.

"You fool!" Regdar shouted. "You moronic bumbler! Do you have any idea what you just did?"

Hennet stuttered out a "no." Regdar grabbed his arm, squeezing so hard that Hennet almost cried out. Regdar looked at Lidda, and the halfling pulled out her dagger and used it to catch the chain. With his free hand, Regdar pulled open a pocket in his tunic, and Lidda dropped the artifact into it.

"Neither do I," said the fighter, releasing Hennet and taking a few cagey steps back, "but I doubt it's good. For all we know, you just made the rift twice as wide and twice as stable, letting Pelor-knows-what through. For all we know, you just doomed us all!"

"Maybe I shut the rift," Hennet shot back, jabbing a finger against the larger man's solid breast. "Did you think of that? At least I did something instead of falling onto my face in a pit trap a toddler could have avoided!"

"Stop it," Sonja and Lidda protested, unheard and unacknowledged.

"What about that boy, Teron?" asked Regdar. "You let him come along with you even though he couldn't fight well enough to defend himself against a single orc. Why? Did he remind you of yourself? You let him get killed."

Stung by the accusation, Hennet cried out, "That's good, coming from the lunatic who rushes into a half a dozen gnolls, hacking every which way without any regard for what his mates might be up to with spells or bows. Acts like an idiot, prevents from anyone helping him, and gets himself knocked out for his trouble. Who wants to literally burn bridges that are our only route of escape. The addle-pated warrior with more weapons than brains, who loses his own lady then lusts after another man's so openly that I feel frankly embarrassed for him."

A roar grew in Regdar's deepest seat of anger, spreading throughout his body, turning his face to a bright scarlet. Veins bulged in his neck and forehead and a string of babble flowed from his mouth, completely beyond his control.

"If I had Sonja then I'd take *some effort* to be more atten- tive to *her*! Neglected in this dungeon the last place she'd want to be in the world as you make jokes! You don't *deserve Sonja* you scrawny little glory-thirsty mageling! If it wasn't for Sonja standing here I'd crush you where you stand."

"Is that all that's stopping you?" Hennet challenged him.

Regdar slammed his right fist across the smaller man's cheek. The unprepared sorcerer flew backward and slammed into the wall, where he knocked over a suit of armor before slumping to the ground. As the armor fell, it triggered a trap in another corner of the room, loosing a barbed arrow that zipped across the room and struck the wall just above Hennet's head then bounced away.

The emotional satisfaction Regdar felt from the punch faded away fast, to be replaced by a deep sense of shame. The world above was freezing, the Plane of Ice threatened to con- sume everything, and he couldn't think of anything but his own pain. What would Sonja think of him now? Could

Hennet forgive him? And what of Lidda, his longest and most faithful companion in travel and adventure? All these faces looked at him with mixtures of shock, anger, and disappointment. All was silent as each waited for the others to speak first.

The stillness was shattered by a huge bang from the next room. The sound echoed repeatedly across the cubic room. Regdar pushed the heavy, black door wider open to peer into the adjoining room, only to have it yanked away from his hand. He found himself looking into the fat, armored torso of a giant. It was hunched over because it was too tall to stand upright in the room. Even stooped, its bald head scraped the black ceiling of the oven. In one arm it clutched a huge, thick club, and in the other it had a triangular shield. The far door was open but intact despite having been forced by this behemoth.

Regdar, Hennet, and Lidda all screamed "frost giant!" Only Sonja knew better. The creature was a verbeeg—smaller than a frost giant but closely related to them, just as evil and almost as dangerous.

The verbeeg swung its club at Regdar. The fighter hopped deftly back and used his foot to pull Hennet's short spear back into the treasure chamber at the same time that grasped the edge of the door with both hands and pulled with all his might. The door slipped from the giant's grasp and noiselessly closed the portal a moment after Regdar whipped his hands back into the treasure room. No sooner had the door closed than they heard an ear-splitting *boom* from the massive club striking the door. It shook the entire room, setting the treasures vibrating and jangling.

"Will the oven room heat up again?" Hennet wondered, pulling himself up and rubbing the welt on his cheek. "That would be an overdue twist of fate in our favor."

"It won't unless the other door closes," said Lidda.

"I don't think it's going to be in there long enough for that to matter," said Regdar as the door shuddered under another crash. A few suits of armor vibrated free of their mounts and clattered to the stone floor. The next impact sounded as if the verbeeg had abandoned its club and was instead slamming itself full-force against the door. The panel wouldn't hold much longer. Regdar tried to reinforce it with his body, and Lidda and Hennet came up to do the same.

"That's a verbeeg," said Sonja from behind. "They're fairly intelligent. Maybe we can reason with it."

The club struck against the door again, knocking Lidda backward with the door's recoil.

"This one doesn't sound especially reasonable," the halfling said, springing back to her feet.

"Get away from the door," Sonja advised, and the others took her advice. They backed away to the corners of the room, weapons drawn and ready to fight. Regdar made sure the Frozen Pendant was secure within his coat and readied his greatsword as the verbeeg struck the door again, and again. The final blow smashed the door inward to hang limply on its bent and torn hinges. The giant bent low and squeezed its head and shoulders through the doorway, preceeded by the menacing club.

"Where is the Pendant!" it bellowed, sweeping the club to and fro, smashing crates and upsetting pedestals. Its Common was oddly accented and deafeningly loud.

Hennet fired a burst of magic at its massive chest. The spell briefly draped the room in sepulchral green. His magic missile slipped around the verbeeg's shield to strike squarely on its chainmail-covered breast. The monster reared back in pain but only slammed against the doorframe. Enraged, it surged forward, tearing out most of the doorjamb and plunging headlong into the treasure chamber.

Regdar and Lidda dired to the floor as the massive club

swept just above their heads. Boxes, vases, picture frames, and rolled tapestries crashed and tumbled across the room. The tumult triggered several traps—arrows and darts launched from hidden points along the walls brought a sharp cry from the verbeeg, which stared dumbly at three metal shafts now buried in its arms and shoulder.

Taking advantage of the distraction, Regdar dashed forward and drove his sword against the wide shield that the verbeeg held before its pendulous belly. The giant responded instinctively by thrusting the shield forward, and almost slammed it against Regdar, but the fighter pulled back in time. Even before it had turned to face the warrior, the verbeeg's club was sweeping around in a powerful swing. Regdar readied himself to parry the blow, but it did no good. The blow was driven by such force that the human and his greatsword were both batted aside. Regdar bounced against the wall, and his sword stayed embedded in the verbeeg's weapon.

The monster would have finished Regdar there and then if not for the crossbow bolt fired by Lidda that sliced into a nerve in its lower leg. The well-placed shot was far more painful than injurious. When it whirled back to find the attacker, Hennet rushed out and pulled Regdar to relative safety behind a mahogany cabinet. From there, Regdar caught a flash of Sonja's blonde hair in one of the room's corners, but Lidda was nowhere to be seen.

"Which of you worms," shouted the verbeeg, "is going to give me this damned pendant?"

"Why do you want it?" came Sonja's voice. Whether because of the strange acoustic properties of the room or druidic magic, the verbeeg could not pin down the source of the sound.

"It will earn me a place in the cold ones' new order—and the chance to crack a few human skulls."

The verbeeg pried Regdar's greatsword from its club and

threw it through the open door into the oven room behind it, where it skidded across the floor with a metallic clash.

"If we could get on the other side of it," Hennet whispered to Regdar, "I could catch it in a web and trap it."

"Why not do it from here?" asked Regdar.

Hennet shook his head. "We'd be trapped along with it."

The verbeeg scanned the damage it had caused, looking for whoever might be hiding in the ruins of the treasure room. Cautious and clever, it had no intention of plunging headlong into a room full of hidden enemies.

In the corner of his eye, Regdar saw Lidda peek out from beneath a collapsed suit of armor and slither across the floor. He gaped as she slipped unnoticed between the verbeeg's legs. The halfling crouched behind the giant, then with a spring, she gripped its chain armor and climbed its back like a monkey ascending a thick tree.

The verbeeg snarled in surprise and dropped its shield to the floor with a clank. Its arms flailed right and left, high and low, as it groped for whatever was crawling on its back. Before it could get hold of the halfling perched precariously on its verbeeg's shoulders, Lidda drew her short sword and spiked it against the side of the giant's head. The blade gashed the monster's ear and scalp, drawing a torrent of blood, but the blade bounced off the thick bone. The verbeeg slapped its free hand against the gushing wound and let out a mighty roar that shook the whole room, then slammed its shoulders backward against the wall.

Lidda had already shifted position, and when the verbeeg hit the wall, she sprang forward off its shoulders into a graceful, two-point landing on a nearby treasure chest. The verbeeg slashed its club aimlessly in her direction, but she had already vanished amid the broken cabinets and fallen treasures.

"We need to draw it farther into the room," Hennet yelled as he rose above the cabinet where he was sheltering.

Another magic missile slammed into the verbeeg's upper body but did little to injure or even distract the giant from its slashed scalp.

Regdar emerged as well. Without his greatsword, he grabbed the giant's fallen shield and shrank behind it against the remains of a shattered cabinet. The verbeeg strode uneasily toward the center of the room then threw caution away. Its club swung indiscriminately, tearing apart whatever it struck.

"Now! Move!" shouted Hennet.

At last Sonja emerged from her corner, leaped up into the verbeeg's face, and launched a brilliant flash before its eyes. The giant instinctively brought both its hands up to its face to shield itself from the dazzling light, dropping its club as it did so.

Seizing the opportunity, three humans and a halfling dashed past the dazed giant. Lidda snatched the torch on her way out. Ducking under a flailing elbow, Regdar saw that the far doorway leading out of the oven room was still open. Recalling the tendency of these doors to close on their own, he shouted a warning to Hennet, who again slid his short spear into the doorway just in case. Regdar scooped up his greatsword from the center of the room as he passed. Panting and battered, they turned back to look at the verbeeg, still smashing its way through the treasure room.

"Back here, ugly!" Hennet yelled at the verbeeg, readying his spell.

The verbeeg started, finally realizing that it was alone in the room. With awkward steps it made its way forward, through the shattered doorway and into the oven room. Lidda's gash still ran with blood. As Hennet let his spell fly, a large, intricate, gossamer web unfolded in the air and attached its corners to each wall and the ceiling with the verbeeg at its center. The giant struggled against the constraining silk, but as it did it only become more entangled. It screamed until the web tightened around its face and silenced it completely.

For a minute they watched the verbeeg laboring vainly against Hennet's spell. There was something pathetic about it, and Regdar stepped forward with his greatsword to end the monster's misery.

"I wouldn't do that," cautioned Hennet. "You might not be able to get the sword back."

"Then how do we kill it?" asked Sonja. "Your spell won't last forever."

"I don't know. Right now, though, I don't want to risk cutting the web or accidentally dispelling it with another effect."

Without warning, the door to the treasure room stirred, rose up from the floor, and wedged itself back into the ruined jamb. Four pairs of eyes turned and looked back at the other door, but it still stood wide open, with Hennet's spear lying in the opening. All of them thought the same thing. If the room would heat up again, that would surely kill the verbeeg.

"Will the heat melt the web and free the verbeeg?" asked Regdar.

"It probably will," Hennet said. "But I don't think it has enough strength left to force the door."

"We could probably kill it with arrows," Regdar said, "but we probably would empty our quivers in the process. Lidda, you're our leader down here. What do you think?"

The halfling walked closer to the enwebbed monster and gave it a hard look. "It's not moving. It could be dead already." She turned back to the others. "We roast it."

"What about the Pendant?" asked Regdar. "If we leave it in here, even if it survives the heat the mephits will have a really hard time retrieving it."

"Will they?" asked Sonja. "They sent the verbeeg. They sent us. I think it's safest in our possession."

The other three nodded in reluctant agreement. When they left the room, the door swung shut behind them. Within minutes, they could feel the heat through the wall.

"How long do you suppose it's been since the Frozen Pendant has been taken out of that room?" asked Lidda.

"Not nearly long enough," said Sonja.

As they marched back through the long hallway, Regdar pulled open his bulging pocket and looked at the Frozen Pendant. Its chill threatened to bore a hole in his side. The artifact shone white as a star, and its imperfect dimensions gave it the rough grace of an uncut gemstone. For an awful moment he fancied he could hear it whispering to him, and he thought that as he stared at it, it stared at back at him. An unwelcome shiver shot down his spine, and he found that he couldn't stand the sight of the thing. He closed his pocket tightly, silently acknowledging that the destruction of this awful object was more important than any of their lives.

They reached the base of the hallway with ease and swiftly climbed the spiral stair back to the large, underground hall above them. The old, familiar chill returned as they left the magical warmth behind, but with memories of the oven room threatening to cook them alive still fresh in their minds, the cold felt like an old friend. Sonja in particular was glad to be free of the narrow passages.

Faced with the ebony door in the side of the cylinder, they

silently drew their weapons and wondered what waited for them on the other side. Regdar took the lead, as the strongest and best-armored of the party. The door creaked as he eased it open.

With his greatsword in one hand and the torch in the other, Regdar strode forward, casting his eyes over the sprawling mall that underlay the wizards' city. The torches that illuminated the hall when they'd first entered were all gone or extinguished. In the less-than-adequate light from the lone torch in Regdar's hand, he could see a dozen monstrous eyes staring at him from the icy murals encircling the cylinders that formed the foundations of the towers above. He wondered if any of those glittering orbs were set in mephit sockets or if they were all icy crystals on the walls.

The familiar debris littered the mall as before, but an unsettling silence hung over the place. With each step forward, Regdar heard its echo through the farthest corners of the mall. Cautiously, the others followed him through the doorway. With slow, deliberate steps on the icy floor, they traced the circumference of the cylinder from which they'd just emerged. Regdar kept his distance from Hennet.

"Are they here?" asked Lidda, holding her crossbow at the ready.

"If they are," Regdar whispered, "they're keeping quiet."

Hennet started. "I thought I heard something." He shook his head, peering into the blackness. "It was . . . I don't know where."

"It could have been an echo," said Sonja.

"I don't think so. It didn't sound like it came from where we are."

"I think I heard it too," Lidda agreed. "It sounded like . . . breathing."

A new sound echoed out from the silence, the distinct flapping of tiny wings.

"It's one of the mephits," said Regdar. "Be ready."

They stood with their backs against the cylinder on the opposite side from the door, looking in the direction of the noise. Lidda raised her crossbow and loosed a bolt that sailed into the dim distance, making a tiny, clinking noise as it struck the far wall. That was followed by the distinctive clinking of a chain and the raking of claws against ice.

Staring into the darkness so intently produced phantom dots of light before Regdar's eyes. He blinked heavily and darted his eyes from side to side. A new pair of eyes flickered in the white torch light, and he was certain they weren't part of one of the ancient murals. Breath came heavily, snorts from a massive nose clouding the air with tiny ice particles. A faint growl rolled in the back of the thing's throat as it strode into the light. It was a great cat, unlike anything that patrolled the world's savannahs. Like the giant scorpion, this was a creature of the Plane of Ice. It resembled a lion in form but not composition. Instead of the familiar, tawny yellow, its fur was shades of white, with a thick mane of shimmering, icy blue. A thick, iron collar encircled its neck, and a length of chain trailed alongside it, clinking as the lion dragged it across the frosted floor. Wiry and powerful, the snow lion drove its claws into the icy floor and reared back, ready to pounce. It let out a mighty roar that blasted throughout the cavernous mall, echoing off the walls and ringing until it was all the warrior could do to not clap his hands over his ears.

Hennet had seen enough. He loosed a magic missile toward the lion. The green spell-bolt struck the creature head-on but did little to slow its drive forward. The adventurers scattered away from the cylinder, not wanting to be pinned against a wall by this mad animal. Only Regdar ran forward to engage the beast, trusting his armor to protect him. He hoped to draw the lion away from the others so they could strike it quickly and safely.

The snow lion leaped on Regdar, knocking the fighter back onto the ground. His helmeted head struck the black floor hard. The lion's chain flailed dangerously, slapping the ground next to Regdar's head and cracking the icy coating where it struck. Regdar skidded backward on the slick floor with the lion digging its claws into his breastplate. Its massive weight kept him pressed against the floor while it reared its maned head and roared into the gloom.

Lidda loosed another crossbow bolt that struck the lion in its neck as it was roaring. The shaft sank deep into the frigid flesh. It whipped its head around, spotted Lidda, and uttered a growl that resonated through Regdar's bones. In a flash it abandoned the pinned fighter and pounced after Lidda. She turned to run, but she'd gone only a few steps before slipping on a slick patch of floor and tumbling forward onto her belly.

As the creature raced after Lidda, Sonja dashed back from her sheltered position behind the cylinder and leaped onto the lion's back. It roared in protest and snapped its head back hoping to buck her off, but the druid clung tightly to the glassy skin stretched tight over icy bones. She attempted to magically calm it, but her spell had no effect. This snow lion was too alien a being to be affected by the same magic that would affect an earthly animal. Sonja released one of her hands to pull her cudgel from her waist, hoping her grip on the lion with her other hand would be sufficient. The lion sensed the opportunity and began leaping and bucking like a mad horse. Sonja was hurled through the air to land on a decrepit table alongside one of the cylinders. The table shattered under her impact, and the lion raced to where she fell, ready to deliver a death blow.

From the shadows, Hennet hurled his short spear. It arced through the air and plunged deep into the lion's side. The enraged beast snapped its jaws at the shaft in a furious effort to dislodge it, but it was too far back along its wiry form. Sonja cracked her cudgel against the lion's face, and the beast drooled some, blue otherworldly equivalent of blood as it turned to face her. She struck again, this time knocking its skull against the nearby cylinder and breaking teeth of solid ice from its mouth. The lion's legs buckled. As it collapsed, Hennet buried the point of his short spear into its frozen brain. With a final twitch the lion expired.

Regdar pulled himself up and walked over to join the others. "If that's the worst of it," he said, "then we should be in the clear."

"That's not the worst," Sonja said. "I suspect they still have Glaze in reserve. That would explain why the dragon didn't kill us when it had the chance—the mephits needed us."

"But Glaze nearly killed Hennet, and it chased me down when I ran for the tower, while you were unconscious," protested Regdar. "Then again, I didn't understand why I made it. I thought Glaze would overtake me for sure. Could it really have been staged?"

"I don't see why not," Sonja said. "White dragons are trainable."

"My store of spells is nearly exhausted," Hennet admitted. "Between Glaze, the mephits, and our tangles with the ver-beeg and this lion thing, I don't know how much magic I can contribute now."

"We heard a mephit before," Lidda reminded them. "It must have unleashed the lion. Where did it go?"

"Through there." Sonja pointed almost exactly above them, to the trapdoor through which Hennet had fallen hours earlier. It was small, but any of them could fit through it.

"Interesting," said Regdar. "They won't expect us to come through there. We could probably pile up enough of this old junk to reach the trapdoor and attack them that way. At least we could get a look at what we're up against."

"Good thought," said Sonja.

Everyone set about collecting the debris for this purpose, scavenging for the more solid desks, tables, and chairs that littered the great hall. Recalling the huge pile of broken wood the mephits froze against the door to the tower they claimed was Glaze's lair, they attempted to prize some of it off but found it solidly resisted their best efforts. Ultimately, they managed to gather a fairly sturdy platform that could support even Regdar's weight. As the tallest of the group, Regdar volunteered to look through the trapdoor. Mounting the platform, he slowly eased the trapdoor open, avoiding the accumulation of snow that fluttered down.

He cautiously craned his neck through the trapdoor and saw the familiar towers of ice, now casting longer shadows as sunset approached. Something felt different about the area above ground, and he couldn't quite identify what it was. Regdar turned in a complete circle and studied the stark, empty city. Neither mephits nor Glaze were in evidence. With an idea in mind, he took a quick look straight up to be sure.

Regdar hopped off the platform and pulled the artifact from his pocket, being careful to hold it only by the chain.

"No one's up there," he announced. "More importantly, I know what happened. I know why the crystal turned white."

Lidda was the first to ask why.

"Before we came down here, the winds were blowing away from the rift, right?" The others nodded furiously.

"Well, now they're blowing inward," Regdar explained. "The wind is blowing madly toward a point in the center of the city, where the rift is."

"Toward it," Hennet repeated. Could it be that his impulsive act had actually saved them, reversing the pendant's effects? "Does that mean that the elemental ice is withdrawing?"

"Regdar," Sonja asked, "did it seem to be blowing faster than before?"

"I couldn't tell," Regdar said.

"Then we must assume that the ice and cold will take as long to leave as they did in coming. That's assuming that the effect will stop at removing the ice it dumped onto our plane and not start sucking in material that's native to our world. Either way, though," Sonja affirmed, "we don't have the luxury of waiting here to find out."

"What do you suggest we do?" asked Regdar.

"We don't know how to use the Frozen Pendant properly," Sonja said. "The ice mephits do. We offer them one last chance to cooperate. If they refuse, we kill them. Glaze, too, if we must. I suspect Glaze watches over the surface from its tower even now."

"How could we close the rift after that?" Hennet asked.

"I'll try again to dispel it," Sonja said, stroking the silver ring from Atupal. "With the effect reversed, the rift may be weaker or at least turned more strongly toward the Plane of Ice. If dispelling doesn't work, then we take the Ilskynarawin back to Atupal, or Klionne or Vasaria or any other city where someone can figure out how to use it. And we pray that we can do this in time."

The others nodded at her plan, though they were concerned about personal matters such as whether they would actually survive a trip back across the frozen landscape.

The druid looked squarely at Regdar. "I want you to stay here with the Frozen Pendant," she declared. "Keep an eye on what happens through the trapdoor if you like, but be prepared to defend the artifact to the death. It cannot fall into the mephits' hands, and I don't want to approach them with it in our possession. This is no reflection on the rest of you, but I think it's probably safest in Regdar's keeping."

Lidda spoke up. "I'm the smallest, the most agile. Why not

give it to me? For that matter, why not take it yourself, Sonja? You could probably get back to the cities fastest if the rest of us don't make it out of here."

"I don't like either idea," Regdar objected. "I'd rather stay and fight next to you if need be. I think that's where I'd be more useful."

"I can understand how frustrating this may be for you. But it has to be this way. The Frozen Pendant is more important than any of our lives. Just what the mephits could do with it, I shudder to contemplate. If we should die," she said, pausing slightly, "take it back down there, where it's magically heated. With luck you can hold them off long enough for the cities to send another group."

Regdar reflected on this. Cowering underground seemed a poor way to await his fate. He prayed to all the good gods that it wouldn't come to that. He didn't have nearly enough provisions to hold out for weeks, especially against a constant barrage of whatever monsters the mephits would send after him. Still, he saw the wisdom in Sonja's plan. The pendant mattered far more than any individual's survival.

"All right," the fighter said, stepping back up onto the platform. "My luck goes with you."

Lidda jumped up next to him and wrapped her thin arms around his leg. She looked up at her friend, teary-eyed. After all their battles fought side by side, this was the first time she really feared that she might never see him again.

Regdar tousled her brown locks. "See you soon," he said.

She pulled away reluctantly and joined the others, marching to the black cylinder that contained their route to the surface. Sonja gave him a last, beautiful smile, and it warmed Regdar's heart.

Left alone then in the dark, except for the tiny slit of fading light shining through the trapdoor, Regdar prayed to all the good gods that this would not be the way he died.

⌒

As they passed through the door to the upward stair, Hennet grabbed a piece of debris and used it to prop open the door. If they needed to retreat downward, every second might matter. The flapping of many wings could be heard above them, as well as the shrieking and hissing that constituted the ice mephits' language.

"They're waiting for us," whispered Lidda as they ascended the first steps.

"The mephits won't attack us first—not while they think we have the pendant."

"Maybe not," Hennet said, "but maybe we should." He patted one of the pockets of his robe. "What about the alchemist fire we found down there? A quick toss and we could rid ourselves of most of these mephits in one blow. You heard how they fear fire."

Sonja shook her head. "Do you want to knock down the tower with them? Or rain fire down on us? Let me take the lead, and keep your spear ready. I expect we'll need it."

When they reached the top of the stairway, weapons in hand, they found a dozen ice mephits crowded into the small room, perched along the magnificent tarrasque carving that was etched into the wall. The mephits were so positioned that the maximum number of them were in front of the black door to the outside.

Each of them looked more less exactly the same, and they all wore the same expression—smug self-satisfaction, with not a trace of surprise at the party's arrival. For some moments both groups stared silently at the other, each expecting, even daring, the other to speak first.

Ultimately, one of the mephits broke the silence. It spoke the words slowly, enunciating each syllable carefully. "Do you have the Ilskynarawin?"

"Your verbeeg didn't take it from us, if that's what you're wondering," Sonja said.

"Or that snow lion you set up down there," Hennet added, clutching his short spear so hard his knuckles were white.

"That's how you repay us for retrieving your artifact?" Lidda asked, waving her sword threateningly at the mephit nearest to her, who was the right height to look her directly in the eye. "You try to have us killed?"

"So you haaave the Ilskynarawin?" another mephit chimed in. "Do you have it?"

"No!" Sonja yelled the word and it echoed through the stairways above and below. "We left it down below. We left it in a room that gets so hot, so infernally hot, that a salamander couldn't survive there."

"As hot as Asmodeus's bowels!" Lidda shouted, sliding the magic torch back into the knot on the wall.

The mephits shuddered at the thought. Such heat was horror.

"It would melt you," Sonja said. "In fact, it would do worse than that. It would reduce you to steam in an instant. You would be vaporized without even leaving a wet spot on the floor. And that's where the Ilskynarawin lies. Go and take it, if you want it badly enough!"

"She liiiies!" one of the enraged mephits screamed. "They all lie! It's here. It's close. I can feeeeel it in my skin!"

Another mephit trilled out a nerve-jangling squeal and took to wing. It swooped toward Sonja, trying to sense, to smell, to perceive the artifact on her. "We must have iiit!" cried the creature.

Sonja swung her cudgel and smashed the mephit head-on. It wasn't killed, but it was badly wounded, with crushed wings. The blow flung it backward to sprawl among its fellows. The mephits gasped, startled by the sudden violence.

"No one will have the Ilskynarawin," Sonja declared, "until we get through that door."

The mephits glanced to and fro at each other.

"Why?" one of them asked, hovering in the air over Hennet's head. The sorcerer pointed his spear at it and jabbed slightly, causing the creature to retreat.

"We just want to see," Hennet cooed, "what's on the other side."

"There's nothiiing to see," hissed another mephit. "Nothing to see."

"We want to see that's there's nothing to see," Sonja replied. "If you don't show us, we'll force our way through. We can and we will."

At that, Hennet tossed his short spear straight at the door. The mephits instinctively dodged away from the weapon. When it struck the hard basalt, the way to the door was clear. With a lunge, Hennet plucked the falling spear before it could clatter to the floor. Swinging their weapons to hold back the mephits, Hennet, Sonja, and Lidda rushed the door and forced it open. A sudden blast of cold assaulted their faces. Outside and in natural light once again, they immediately swung round to face the door, ready to slam it shut in the mephits' faces.

Before they could do that, a half dozen or more mephits swarmed the doorway and loosed their icy breath, pelting their enemies with stinging shards of ice that gushed from their mouths and shattered against the backs of Sonja, Lidda and Hennet. The pain and the cold were dulled by their heavy coats, so that the shock of the attack was the worst of it. That was sufficient, however, to knock them sprawling to the ground, unable even to keep their grips on their weapons.

The mephits swept through the doorway, ready to mercilessly slaughter the nearly helpless trio as they scrambled for their weapons. Before the first blow could fall, another voice rang out from across the stark, snow-covered field.

"Halt!"

Regdar stood almost precisely in front of the rift, that point toward which flew all of the snow swirling above them. He hadn't drawn his greatsword, but rather he held his right fist high above his head.

"Observe your precious trinket!" Regdar shouted. He opened his fist and out fell the Ilskynarawin, glowing like a tiny sun, dangling on the gold chain tightly wrapped around his fingers. The mephits ceased their assault on Hennet, Sonja, and Lidda entirely, giving them time to reclaim their weapons and pull themselves to their feet.

Those mephits that were in the air drifted to the ground. All of them stared at the precious artifact they coveted so completely. A reverent silence fell over the nameless city, broken only by the ever-present rush of wind.

"What is he doing?" whispered Hennet to the others. Lidda shook her head in puzzlement, but a wide smile crossed Sonja's features.

Regdar turned around, the Frozen Pendant still clutched firmly in his fist, until he almost faced the rift itself but could still keep his eyes on the mephits. A look of hard resolve covered his face, mixed improbably with the expression of a schoolboy about to do something altogether naughty.

"If you want it . . ." he yelled as he began swinging the pendant. The mephits let out a collective shriek as they realized what was happening.

". . . come and get it!"

Regdar released the pendant. It flew directly into the portal, traveling only a few feet before it vanished in thin air before him. The mephits' collective screeching increased in pitch as they saw their prize disappear and realized how terribly they'd been cheated.

Then they raged.

The Frozen Pendant's principal power was to open a hole into the para-elemental Plane of Ice from the Prime Material Plane, allowing a torrent of ice and cold to blast through. The mephits understood that there was perhaps only one place in all the multiverse where this power was wholly and utterly neutralized.

That was precisely where Regdar had sent it—the Plane of Ice.

Regdar pulled his greatsword from its scabbard and readied himself for the expected onslaught of mephits. After their shriek faded, however, they stood eerily still, all staring at Regdar with their tiny jaws hanging open in shock and disbelief. A new imperative rang through their collective mind. They needed to go back through the rift. They needed to find the artifact and bring it back through to this plane.

That meant getting past Regdar. Only getting past him wasn't good enough. He needed to be slain for what he'd done. In blind anger, just as Regdar had hoped, they emptied the strongest weapon in their collective arsenal directly at him.

The missiles that streaked from their breasts toward Regdar weren't green like Hennet's but shades of orange and red, the colors of fire that the mephits so despised. Their blasts rocketed across the white field, and for a brief moment Regdar contemplated letting himself fall backward through the rift to escape them. Fortunately, he decided it was best to stay in the plane he knew. The missiles slammed weakly against his breastplate. The flurry of impacts pushed him backward, but he knew that if he kept his footing he would be safe.

One of the mephits nearest him tried to take advantage of Regdar's brief distraction to slip right past him into the rift, swooping down from above. It was a good plan with one lethal flaw. However it approached, the mephit needed to dive to Regdar's level to get through the rift itself. When it drew close, Regdar swung his heavy weapon upward, catching its wings and sending it tumbling to the ground. It opened its mouth to cry for help, but no sound came out before Regdar struck the tiny blue head from the body.

At this spectacle, the other mephits took to the air, too, flying through the swirling snow on straining wings, screeching as loudly as they could. Lidda fired her crossbow into the sky, hoping that she might strike one in the mass, while Hennet and Sonja rushed to aid Regdar in defending the rift.

With a reptilian roar and rush of cold air that altered the flow of the wind momentarily, Glaze swooped past and alighted on the side of his tower lair. Quickly he scrambled about, pointing his head down the tower in preparation for launching himself into another pass. In their earlier encounter, the dragon had nearly collided with the ground when forced to perform this maneuver unexpectedly. He knew better this time, and he understood that even his mighty wings were no match for the zephyrs howling toward the rift. This time he scuttled almost to the ground, below the wind, before launching himself from the tower toward Regdar. The warrior faced him with sword raised, ready for the dragon to burst across the far side of the rift like a juggernaut.

"I know what he's doing," Sonja mumbled.

The dragon intended to chase, or if necessary carry, Regdar from his place guarding the rift. This would give the mephits a chance to slip through to the other side and reclaim the Ilskynarawin.

"Stand guard here," she said to the others when they were assembled before the rift. Even as she spoke, the dragon was dropping from the tower. "Hold this position no matter what. I'll take care of Glaze. By the way," she added, "you may want to shield your ears."

"Why?" asked Regdar.

Sonja had no time to answer. Her robes clung to her form, her hair rose and crackled, and the sharp smell of a brewing storm filled the air as electricity arced over the cold ocean of blue in Sonja's eyes. A second later, a blinding zigzag of light flashed down from the clouds above, simultaneously with a deafening thunderclap that resonated against the far towers and echoed down the valley. The perfectly aimed lightning bolt blasted the young dragon out of the air. Glaze plummeted to the snowy plaza like a side of beef. Mephits scattered in all directions, cowering away from the noise and the brightness of Sonja's heartstopping spell.

Regdar and Hennet, too, almost lost control of their instincts and dived for cover, but Lidda smiled calmly at the display, which put all powderworks she'd witnessed to shame. Lightning from a snowstorm was possible after all. Sonja had proved it.

The air was curiously calm after the burst, and so was Sonja. Her hair and clothes hung limp, yet she seemed energized. Eyes blazing, fingertips glowing, she appeared every inch a witch of nature as she turned her stare on Glaze.

The dragon was not dead. From a crumpled tangle of wings and tail and neck, he sprang into a catlike crouch, tattered wings folded sleekly against his flanks. He would not fly again without months of rest and recuperation to his damaged wings. Pale, purple eyes flared at Sonja, matching the druid's gaze in intensity and anger.

"Don't let the mephits through," Sonja whispered to the others. "Guard the rift. Guard it no matter what happens."

She ran from them and from the rift, racing across the field of snow toward one of the towers. As she did, Glaze trotted after her on all fours, issuing a rasping cry in her wake.

Hennet or Regdar might have protested Sonja's actions or raced to her aid except that the mephits saw their opportunity as well and assailed the rift's defenders in mass. They swooped in as groups then pulled back at the last moment. Over and over they rushed forward, group after group, probing for an opportunity to strike without suffering a counterattack. If they could provoke Regdar into swinging his sword, or Hennet into thrusting his spear, all the better. Lidda stood between the two men, firing crossbow bolts at the mephits which all too rarely found their marks as the creatures zipped and zagged through the air.

In all this, Hennet and Regdar avoided sharing any eye contact. An obvious red welt had risen where Regdar struck Hennet. In the cold air, the pain had settled down to a dull sting, an all-too-persistent reminder of what had happened between them down below.

Regdar unexpectedly let go of his heavy sword, letting it fall to the ground with a thud. "I think," he said, "one of those mephits must be using that ability Sonja told us about."

"You mean your armor's gone cold?" asked Lidda. She ran a hand over Regdar's breastplate and pulled it away. The visible metal was frosted over and was growing still colder.

"We need to get the armor off you," Hennet said.

Regdar shook his head. "Don't let your guard down. I can't move my arms now. My armor's locked in place. I can't fight while this lasts. I'm sorry. Look to yourselves."

"It's frigid!" Lidda said. "Don't tell me you can take that."

"I have to," Regdar replied through chattering teeth. "Anyway, I think I'm getting used to it."

Sonja, meanwhile, was letting the irate, snarling Glaze chase her around the towers, playing a dangerous game of hide-and-seek with the dragon to keep Glaze from getting a clear blast at her with his breath. She could feel the static electricity regenerating in the storm above, and she knew that soon she could use this to draw down another lightning bolt. There was no way the dragon could stand another shot of that sort. Sonja only needed to keep it occupied until then.

She was getting tired. The cold invigorated her, and the open air felt like liberation after the tight passageways down below, but this blast of energy slowly faded as days of exhaustion caught up with her. Sweat trickled down Sonja's cheeks, and she felt a lump of fear in her throat. She could hear Glaze trotting after her, claws scraping on the ice.

Rage gave Glaze energy. With his wings too badly damaged for flight, the dragon was reduced to something akin to a massive, mad dog, chasing its prey round and round the icy towers. Sonja wove and dodged the relentless pursuit. She managed to stay about one tower ahead of the dragon at all times, but she was tiring and Glaze was not.

The others were too busy fending off the mephits to keep track of Sonja, and doubly so since Regdar's incapacitation. As one mephit dived for the rift, hoping to take advantage of Regdar's inaction, Hennet jabbed at it with his short spear. The mephit was too far away, but it was leery of the spear and pulled back. Lidda had quickly learned that the moment when they drew back was the mephits' weakness. The abrupt change of direction forced them to drastically slow their flight. As the creature stopped short of Hennet's spear, it hung motionless in the air for just a moment—long enough for Lidda to launch a crossbow bolt through its belly. It shrieked as it tumbled down onto the point of Hennet's spear. The sorcerer thrust upward, neatly impaling the creature. He flicked it forward quickly, dislodging the body with great force so that it sailed halfway across the field.

"That's what'll happen to the rest of you," Hennet shouted, eyeing the mephits through the thin haze of his own misty breath.

"How are you doing?" Lidda asked Regdar.

Regdar didn't reply. His teeth were clenched behind taut, blue lips. Moisture around his tightly squeezed eyes froze into tiny, white pearls of ice. He wanted to scream against the metallic cage of cold formed by his armor, but he refused with Hennet present. He stood rigid as a golem, his flesh freezing and burning, and waited an eternity for the cold to fade.

Across the field, Sonja's energy was running out. She felt her legs ready to buckle beneath her, and she could not yet call down another lightning bolt. Slipping behind a tower still crusted in a thick layer of ice, she put her faith in a spell that had saved her parents countless times on the Endless Glacier. Her entire form became the white of snow, and she slipped up against the tower's side.

A minute, she thought, maybe two, then the lightning will have gathered its strength for another strike. Then the dragon would die. Glaze was born on the tundra, too, with great intuition about his native surroundings, but the dragon was not smart. He reacted out of instinct. Sonja used this to lure Glaze away from the rift.

Now she was in a position where Glaze's instincts could prove deadly. There might be no fooling such a creature, no hiding from his heightened senses. She flattened herself as best she could against the icy tower, hoping desperately that her ruse would keep her invisible long enough.

When Glaze emerged around the tower, it was the first time Sonja got a good look at the creature. He limped, and his left wing was in tatters. The beast stopped and growled. Sonja left no footprints on the ice, yet Glaze somehow knew she hadn't gone past here. He could smell her presence in the air. Like a scaly bloodhound he sniffed the air, trying to trace the druid's path. He looked up to see if she somehow climbed the tower, then clawed the ground in frustration. Dismayed, the dragon began pacing round the tower, scouring every inch for his wayward prey.

Glaze picked a random section of the tower, stared at it intensely, and then slashed it with his claws and snapped at it with his jaws. Content that this wasn't the spot, he moved on and repeated those actions a few feet farther on. Sonja meticulously shifted her way round the tower, moving imperceptibly ahead of the searching dragon.

The dragon stopped in his tracks and cast a look at her location. She stopped, standing very still. Slowly, deliberately, the dragon moved in her direction. Glaze's throat rumbled and his eyes were riveted directly on Sonja's invisible form. He knew exactly where she was. Sonja was sure of that. She was trapped, and she would live only until the dragon opened his jaws.

A single mephit swooped close to the rift, staying just out of the reach of Hennet's spear. It hurled incoherent curses and taunts as it dodged Lidda's crossbow bolts.

"Tell your friends they can give up," Hennet advised the mephit. "We'll never let you through."

"Your Pendant is gone for good," Lidda said.

"Whaaat say you, large one?" it hissed at the unmoving Regdar. "Is iiit too cold for you?"

Regdar could hold back no longer. He opened his mouth and let out an agonized yowl. As he did, he bent down, armor squealing in protest, and grabbed his greatsword off the ground. An upward slash struck the unprepared mephit directly between the legs and sliced completely through its body. The mephit fell into halves before their eyes.

"You're all right!" Lidda cried.

"Not yet," said Regdar as he straightened his back painfully. "I think I'm just too cold to feel how bad it really is."

⌇⌇⌇

Glaze plunged a talon at Sonja's location and she pulled slightly to the right. He snapped at her and she shifted slightly to the left. She realized that she lived only by virtue of the dragon's playful malice. In the sky above she saw static electricity dancing among the clouds, and she felt its strains moving through her own bones, awaiting her command. At last she gauged that she could draw down another lightning bolt, but now it was too late and the dragon was too close. She needed distance between herself and Glaze.

Sonja bolted from the tower in a great burst of speed. Her spell of concealment faded as she raced right past Glaze. Immediately the dragon was after her as she charged toward the rift, but she had intentionally run to his right, knowing the beast would have a harder time turning away from his injured side. She ran and ran, and when she was sure she had enough distance between herself and Glaze she stopped and whirled to launch her spell.

As she did, a well-placed mephit exhaled a blast of ice along the back of her head and neck. Its breath would have constituted little more than a nuisance in another circumstance, but the unexpected assault broke the druid's concentration and scuttled her spell. Lightning flashed down from the storm but without Sonja's direction. It struck randomly, disintegrating an unfortunate mephit and melting the ice within a ten-foot radius. A splash of steaming water struck the mephit that attacked Sonja and instantly dissolved its wings and half its body. The creature flopped to the ground where it squealed in agony until the warm liquid melted it completely.

Undeterred, Glaze bounded headfirst into Sonja, knocking her backward into the snow. She reached for her cudgel to strike back, but the dragon was quicker. He unleashed the full force of his powerful breath onto her. Her hand jutted forward in an instinctive but useless act of self defense. The dragon's breath buffeted her with an awesome mix of freezing air, gale-force wind, and icy magic. She was wrapped in a cocoon of cold, unable to breathe or see. Searing waves of cold pierced the core of her being. When she tried to scream, her throat filled with ice. She tried to struggle, but ice bound her limbs in place. A white field wrapped across her eyes, burned her face, shut her off from the world.

Exalting, Glaze moved in for the kill. Mephits flanked him, several alighting on the dragon's back or hovering next to his shoulders, all of them hissing in glee at the ice druid's impending death.

Across the field, still standing guard before the rift, Hennet looked at Lidda, Lidda looked at Regdar, and Regdar looked at Hennet. Each sought some sort of encouragement or dissuasion. They needed confirmation that the plan could be changed, that they had to fight for everyone's life. Most of all, they had to agree that letting Sonja die that way would serve no higher purpose.

Abandoning their positions at the rift might be wrong,

but no matter the consequences, it was what they needed to do.

As one they sprang across the field toward Glaze and Sonja. Hennet launched a magic missile, the last he had prepared, and it struck the dragon's side. Glaze turned away from Sonja to face the new threat instead. The mephits flew away and winged their way toward the rift, cackling delightedly to each other. This had been their hope all along. But none of the advancing heroes turned back to watch the mephits vanish through the undefended rift into the Plane of Ice.

Glaze sucked in a mighty breath, but then his targets scattered, leaving the monster unsure where to attack. Regdar veered to the right, Hennet to the left, and Lidda kept coming straight on. Confounded, Glaze lunged toward the smallest foe, but the halfling dived into the snow. She slid under the dragon and slashed her sword upward as she went, drawing blood from Glaze's tender underbelly. Hennet drove his spear through the dragon's already-damaged wing and sliced with it, and Regdar slashed at the scaly, flailing tail.

The dragon snarled, clawed, twisted, and roared, railing against his assailants. Lidda sank her sword deeper into Glaze's belly. Hennet stabbed his spear into the side of the dragon's neck, bringing a steady stream of blood that pulsed like a tiny geyser. Shocked and howling with pain, Glaze made a last attempt to escape. Jumping, whirling, spinning uncertainly, he spilled dragon blood across the white field until the ground was cloaked like a red carpet.

Recovering his wits at last, Glaze gathered his limbs beneath him and set himself to bound free of his attackers. In the moment when the dragon was coiled and motionless, Regdar's greatsword stabbed into his flank just ahead of Glaze's right haunch. The blade sliced forward through flesh and ribs until entrails tumbled free. The dragon roared, firing a blast of icy power straight up into the sky then down into the ground with such force that the frozen paving stones buckled. His attackers scrambled away from the flailing limbs. Thrashing and writhing, Glaze raged against the pain until the beast finally lay still. Within moments, frost coated the gory heap.

Hennet, Regdar, and Lidda didn't spare a minute on the spectacle of the dead dragon. When they turned to look at Sonja, they saw her emerge from the cocoon of ice. She was transformed, no longer a frail human in a hostile environment but master of the element glorying in its strength. Her pale cheeks were streaked with lines of fiery red. She clutched her cudgel in a fist rimed with ice, and glittering crystals scattered from her blonde hair, to be carried on the wind toward the yawning rift.

They faced her almost sheepishly, having violated her orders to guard the rift no matter what, but there was neither disappointment nor blame in her voice, only determination.

"None of you must follow me now," she said. Her voice rang with icy, otherworldly detachment. "None of you could survive where I must go. This time, your own lives depend on you obeying my command."

With that, she turned toward the rift. Her white robes fluttered and crackled like ice as she ran and jumped. A white flash outlined the invisible rift, and she was gone.

For long moments they stood gazing at the spot of air where she disappeared. Eventually Regdar said, "We must still guard the rift. If any of the mephits find the pendant, they'll try to come back through. It's up to us to kill them before they can do any more damage."

Lidda agreed, but Hennet said nothing. He was lost in his own thoughts.

"Hennet?" Lidda asked, tugging at his leg.

The sorcerer looked down on the halfling and put his hand on her head.

"I'm sorry," he told her.

Hennet turned to Regdar, meeting his eyes for the first time since their feud in the treasure room, and said, "I have to know."

At that, he too rushed through the rift, vanishing into the cold oblivion.

"Hennet, don't!" Lidda shouted but too late. She clutched Regdar's hand. "Regdar, we have to go after him. He'll die in there!"

Regdar shook his head. His first instinct was to say, "Some of us have to be smart," but he thought of Naull and what he would have done, months ago in the City of Fire, if a portal had existed linking him to her. With that memory in mind, he gauged his words more carefully. Instead, he said, "Hennet made his own choice, as surely as Sonja has."

All they could do was wait.

A world of white.

So it seemed to Hennet, as if the entire world had faded away and been replaced with only whiteness. As a little boy it had always bothered him, that moment of winter when the sky and the land lined up in color so precisely that the horizon could not be identified, so that ground and air ceased to be separate entities but merged and transformed into a vast gray-white waste. This place, the unloved pocket of the multiverse Sonja called the Elemental Plane of Ice, was a thousand times worse.

The ground beneath his feet was rock solid but white. Hennet wondered if there was any real surface land on this plane at all or only ice on ice. The air was filled with tiny, white particles, something akin to snowflakes but more jagged and hostile. To Hennet's horror, they weren't falling. They hovered in the air, perfectly still and stable, kept in place by forces Hennet could not even guess at. As he waved his hand through the air, they melted away from the heat brought by proximity to his flesh. Above, he could see through this forest of ice an indifferent, bluish glow which seemed to emanate from all parts of an apparently sunless sky. This was all he could see. His vision was so impaired by the impenetrable weather that he could not see Sonja, the ice mephits, or the rift through which he just came.

He felt no wind. Hennet half-expected the Plane of Ice would be forever wracked by the same howling winds that demolished the Fell Forest, but at this moment at least there was instead an unearthly quiet over the place, a hush that Hennet did not find peaceful at all but deeply unsettling.

What of the rift? he wondered. On the other side it blew fiercely as the elemental material was sucked back into this plane, but here? Perhaps it didn't blow spectacularly with wind and fury but simply diffused its essence back into the Plane itself.

Hennet stood, short spear at the ready, puzzled about what to actually do. Ice from the ground crept up his legs and coated them in a sheen of frost. The air itself, the jagged snowflakes that stared at him so menacingly, came closer, clinging to his face and his hair and his arms and his torso.

His blood froze.

He couldn't imagine the air being colder than what he'd faced these last days in the cold zone, but the Plane of Ice knew temperatures far below even the coldest, most remote recesses of the Endless Glacier, where neither man nor mammoth nor frost giant ever dared set foot. Water froze. Flesh froze. Ice froze. To Hennet it seemed that no creature, not even Sonja, not even the mephits, could survive for long in so harsh a place as this. This for him was the wellspring of all cold, the ultimate source not only of the plague of ice that now threatened Atupal and Klionne but of all winters, all frosts, all sudden cold spells that kill crops and children alike. It was the evil of cold and the cold of evil.

So Hennet thought as the harsh chill penetrated his

bones, and all thoughts left him but for a distant yearning for the comforts of a place by the hearth and two warm arms enfolding him.

"Hennet!"

The name echoed through this strange world, striking the sorcerer with the force of a magic missile to his brain. He shook off the ice that settled on his limbs and jogged painfully in the direction of the voice, pushing his way through the icy particles that clung to the air. Peering through the frozen fog hanging all around him, he desperately searched for the source of the sound.

"Sonja!" he yelled as loudly as he could, shaking frost off his vocal cords. He heard the fluttering of wings swooping past him and instinctively whirled about to face it, but he saw nothing. There Hennet stood, once again inert and unsure of where to turn next.

"Keep moving! If you stand still, you'll freeze in moments," the welcome female voice cried again. "Come to the sound of my voice! We must keep them from getting the Pendant!"

Where is the pendant? Hennet wanted to shout as he forced his way through the sluggish air, but all he could produce was an inarticulate string of random syllables. In the icy silence, he faintly heard the mephits' wings beat as they flew above him, doubtless scanning for their unholy prize. In a flash he knew what he had done wrong. He should have stood guard at the opening of the rift to block them from getting back in with the pendant.

Only he knew he wasn't here for the pendant.

Hennet thought he heard wings close by, and he whirled again. He gulped with glee as the tip of his spear impaled a mephit, which let out a cry of pain and crashed to the ground. Tiny ice crystals swirled riotously in its wake, forming whorls and kaleidoscopic swirls above the corpse.

"You killed one of them!" Sonja confirmed a gleeful voice from the frozen fog, and Hennet again was on the move, desperate to find the source of her calls. But he felt the sluggishness closing in on him. He heard his joints crack as he moved, as if he was freezing from the inside out.

There was no warmth in him now, no warmth anywhere in existence. His exposed skin turned white, and his hair stood up, dagger-stiff. Mentally he conjured up images of roaring, crackling fires, hot food and drink, and Sonja's welcome touch. He even wished he was back under the city in the oven room. He almost died there, but the torment of having his blood turned to steam seemed far better than freezing to ice. He yelped in horror as he realized he could no longer feel his hands. He could see them, but otherwise he had no way of being certain they existed. His legs were not far behind.

Hennet's cloak was partly frozen, and bits of it crackled and snapped off as he walked. He'd sometimes wondered what freezing to death would be like. Some said that it was the least painful of deaths, a gradual, gentle loss of feeling, like a slow drift into sleep. He knew now that was lie. He would gladly exchange this death for any other. He blinked, and frost clung to his eyelashes. When he breathed heavily, his breath froze in midair. The tiny crystals joined the swirl of others that danced round his head. White oblivion threatened to envelop him forever.

There it was. Glistening brighter than any diamond in the pale blue light, the ice-white jewel of the Ilskynarawin, the Frozen Pendant itself. Hennet was struck by how small and insignificant it looked—in the face of this eternity of snow, a tiny chunk of whiteness possessed so much power. It lay where it landed, launched through the rift by Regdar's toss, its golden chain half covered by the snow. It looked different here on this plane that was the source of its power but paradoxically where it was useless. It was larger and shone brighter, making it more visible in the diminished light, and it had transformed from a misshapen lump into a perfect sphere of purest white. It glowed serenely, perfectly untroubled by all that happened. For a moment, Hennet stood, looking at the Frozen Pendant at his feet as if it dared him to pick it up and claim it, and he hesitated to accept the challenge.

He wondered for a moment if he should call Sonja. She'd know what to do with it. But he could still hear the mephits beating their wings above him, and he knew he didn't dare give away its location. He needed to do this himself.

Hennet's bones creaked as he bent over, slowly extending his hand to grasp the necklace.

Before he could reach it, a mephit burst out of the fog above him. With lightning speed it swooped down, snatching the pendant away just before Hennet's hand could close around it. For half an instant it turned to Hennet, smiled, and hissed at him, before setting its wings flapping and vanishing into the air.

Hennet screamed in frustration, but no sound passed his stiffened lips. He tried to toss his short spear after the mephit, but he couldn't move fast enough to hurl the weapon effectively. It wobbled only a few yards before flopping to the ground. Hennet felt his legs crack and collapse underneath him. He, too, tumbled onto the ground. With great effort he rolled onto his back and lay staring up at the diamond-cold, heartless sky. Here, with whatever time was left to him, he contemplated his failure as the cold soaked into his organs. In short order, he knew, the mephits would return to the Prime and with the coveted Ilskynarawin in their claws they would cement and expand the rift so that pure, unfiltered, elemental ice would spill over into his world. Regdar and Lidda would fight, but the new blast of ice would be more than any humans could endure. Before long Klionne and Atupal would fall and the lands beyond would face a terrible, new threat. All mankind would be in danger. He had failed Sonja utterly.

There was nothing he could do to stop it.

He remembered how the tiny crystals of ice melted away from his hand when he first stepped through the rift. Raising his hand, he saw that it no longer happened. The crystals collected on his skin, forming a shell. Even the tiny bit of heat required to melt these specks was beyond his body's ability to generate. What damage a fireball would do here! he mused. But he was too weak; he was dying. He wished momentarily that he still had the fire wand he'd used against the elemental ice scorpion. That would be something to see.

Hadn't he found something else . . . not a spell, but a magical flame? Was it a memory or only a wish becoming illusion?

Numb hands rummaged clumsily through his clothes, searching. When he bumped against the flask in his pocket, the memory came back. Alchemist fire! Regdar had found it on the corpse in the pit. Hennet fished out one of the flasks with great effort looked at it, trying to concentrate. Did he really want to do this? It could kill him . . . but he was dying anyway.

It could kill Sonja if she was too close to the blast. She had opposed him using fire magic all along, and she'd been right.

How could he risk killing the woman he loved now that she was just realizing her potential? He recalled her words about heroism, about the heroes of legend who achieved great things because they left their personal concerns behind them. "They were not people and neither must we be." Was that the foundation of heroism? All his life Hennet had wanted to become a legend. Now he had the opportunity, and no one would survive to spread the tale of his sacrifice.

With all the strength he could muster, Hennet tossed the

flask of alchemist fire. He was surprised at how far his stiffened limbs managed to propel it. The sticky fluid inside the flask would ignite on contact with air. All it needed was to burst open and it would set off a firestorm that just might destroy the rift, or at least kill mephit that had claimed the pendant—if it broke. Hennet lost track of it amid the swirling particles, but the cold alone was sufficient to shatter the fragile glass.

The plane itself moaned at the flash of unwelcome heat. Hennet shielded his eyes but gloried in the warmth as the blast rolled across him. The explosion was far beyond what a vial of alchemist fire would have caused on the Prime Material Plane, for fire was an alien force here, unknown and unchecked. The ground buckled, and the sky warped under the stress of fantastic heat. The frozen fog vanished altogether, revealing the endless, wan expanse for just a moment before it was concealed again by clouds of steam that roiled upward and outward only to solidify and rain down as solid ice.

The mephits closest to the blast were instantly vaporized by the waves of fire. These were the fortunate ones. Those farther away screeched in agony as the terrifying flames licked at them and they witnessed their bodies melting into puddles beneath them. Hennet watched a mephit plummet from the sky after its wings melted from its back. It plunged into a steaming pool of boiling water, where it disappeared in a hiss of vapor.

Hennet could see the rift now, for the slow but steady stream of icy material that oozed through from the Prime had been the same color as the pervasive, frozen fog. The rift looked smaller on this side than on the other. What's more, it appeared weaker. Strain was apparent. He could see how precarious was the balance of forces that maintained the conduit. It shuddered under the weight of the elemental material passing through it. Its designers never expected it to be attacked from this side. Hennet hoped that meant Sonja would have a better chance to dispel it from here.

The Ilskynarawin, no longer the Frozen Pendant since its golden chain melted in the blast of heat, tumbled from the sky and landed with a splash in the center of the cleared area, which was now covered by a shallow pool of steaming water. Hennet couldn't move his damaged limbs, he could only watch as four surviving mephits swept down from the sky, desperate to recapture the treasure. He groped for another flask of alchemist fire, but his hands, both frozen and burned, could feel nothing. He feared his last gesture might have been in vain.

He wondered: where was Sonja?

His heart leaped when he spotted her, wrapped in white, sweeping out of the vapor toward the rift. She plunged across the wet landscape like a pale ghost, little more than a white flash. No sooner did one of the mephits alight near the Ilskynarawin than Sonja was upon it. Her cudgel cracked against the creature's skull with such force that the body shattered. Hennet watched in awe. Reborn by the dragon's ice cocoon, Sonja was the master of these creatures even on their own plane.

Another mephit caught Sonja with its frigid breath, but she ignored it. The water on the ground was rapidly freezing around the Ilskynarawin. The frozen fog crept in. Sonja cast a wary glance upward before crushing the second mephit with her cudgel.

That provided enough distraction, however, for another mephit to slip behind her and free the glimmering Ilskynarawin from its icy cage. Taking to the air, it raced urgently to reach the rift ahead of the druid.

To get through, Sonja knew the mephit would have to swoop low, just as on the other side. If she could get there first, she could stop it, but she couldn't get to the rift first. For an awful moment it looked as if the mephit would make its escape. It flew down, headed straight for the rift.

With deadly aim, Sonja threw her cudgel. The club struck the mephit in the back, causing it to lose its grip on the Ilskynarawin and propelling it headlong through the rift. It vanished with a tiny flash, and when it didn't sweep back through a second or two later, Sonja silently thanked Regdar and Lidda.

She pounced onto the artifact as a third mephit swept low above it, blasting her again with its breath. The druid held tightly onto the Ilskynarawin and punched upward. Her fist demolished the mephit's head, and its body tumbled to a heap yards away.

Moving as casually as if she was in her own garden, Sonja retrieved her weapon. With the deadly cudgel in one hand, the coveted artifact in the other, and the rift silently oozing ice behind her, she offered a challenge to the lone, surviving mephit—if you want it, come take it from me. For half a minute or more the creature hovered, searching the ice druid's eyes for any hint of weakness or wavering of resolve. Finding none, it decided to leave with its life. As it turned away, Sonja leaped after it. Her club smashed down with terrific strength, and the mephit crumbled.

With her enemies dead, Sonja rushed to Hennet, who stared semiconscious up to the sky as the advancing ice threatened to overtake him. As her face came into his view, beaming with a mixture of victory and concern, the edges of Hennet's mouth curled stiffly into an approximation of a smile.

"My love," she said softly, kneeling next to him. Keeping the Ilskynarawin close, Sonja expended all of her healing and protection spells in an effort to keep Hennet with her. Then she took him in her arms and carried his limp body to the rift. Along the way, she recovered his short spear and slipped it safely into his robes.

She did not weep as she looked down on his pale face and kissed his cold forehead. She knew he would live and recover, but she also knew she would never see him again. Fate and nature gave her a different path.

One more thing remained to do. She ran her hands through Hennet's robes. The cloth cracked and fell away in pieces as she sought her prize—the two remaining flasks of alchemist fire. They were frozen solid, but thawed they might work again. Hennet had proven their power in this place.

Gently, she pushed the sorcerer's inert form toward the rift. He floated for just a moment before disappearing with a white flash.

Alone on the blasted expanse of ice, Sonja extended her hand—the one that wore the silver ring from Atupal, with one more dispelling charge. She extended it toward the rift, closed her eyes, and let the magic work.

It happened more easily than she expected. There was none of the mental battle she'd faced when she tried, vainly, to dispel the rift from the other side. The portal slipped shut as easily as any wooden door, leaving no trace of itself behind. With the rift extinguished, there was no way for Sonja to return. She was trapped.

Sonja removed the now-useless ring from her finger and cast it away. This was not a perfect solution, she reflected. Much elemental ice remained on the Prime Material Plane. The damage was considerable, and there was no quick, magical fix for it. She knew that in time, nature itself would reverse the harm.

Around her, the damage caused by Hennet's blast of alchemist fire was all but repaired. She was glad, for this place was nature, too, and it also required protection from radical disruptions. That would be her work from now on. Just as her parents protected the natural order of the Endless Glacier, she would do the same here. All that remained of the flame damage was a slender sinkhole where the water of the melted ice collected, and it was about to freeze over. Into this Sonja dropped the Ilskynarawin and watched the evil artifact sink to untold depths where, she sincerely hoped, no one would ever look for it again.

Sonja turned and regarded the sunless, summerless mass of her new home. To survive here, she knew she would have to shed all of the civilization she'd picked up in the southlands. Shed it, but not forget it. She would never forget Hennet, Regdar, and Lidda.

Sonja extended her arms and slowly transformed into a huge black wolf. In this wild form she ran into the mists of the frozen distance.

Epilogue . . . Hennet floated through a disoriented, half-waking state of restless motion, of endless up-and-down movement, cradled and carried. At one point, Hennet was sure that he opened his eyes long enough to see the land still carpeted in implacable snow, and he lamented that they failed. But eventually he felt warmth on his cheek, warmth from Pelor's sun, and he knew that they had won. They were heroes. They had turned back the tide of ice and saved Klionne, Atupal, and only the gods knew how many cities beyond them.

But they lost the girl.

When he awoke, Hennet was wrapped in an envelope of silk with the welcome aromas of incense and wood smoke wafting through the air. He felt soft, lingering pain, but most of all, he felt warm.

"You're awake," said a familiar, female voice.

"Lidda," said Hennet, squinting. He lay in an unfamiliar bed, his head resting on a luxurious feather pillow in a cozy, oak-lined room. The halfling sat next to him in a rocking chair that was so grotesquely oversized for her that he couldn't help smiling. A small table stood next to the bed. A good-sized fire kept a steady roar in the hearth in the corner.

"It's good to have you back," Lidda said.

"Where is this?" Hennet asked.

"Atupal. The Berron Inn. You've been sleeping for days."

"Regdar?

"He carried you all the way here. When we arrived," Lidda explained, "we had you healed at the shrine of Pelor. The priest said that you were probably a few hours from death."

"Gods above," Hennet mouthed. He felt stiff and weak but knew he been healed. The frostbite that destroyed his flesh on the Plane of Ice was gone. It was strange, though, that he could still feel the bruise on his cheek where Regdar had punched him. Perhaps it was all in his mind, he thought.

Hennet pulled himself up in bed and peeked out the window. Some snow still clung to the rooftops of Atupal, but the summer sun was doing its work.

"So the cold zone did reach this far," he observed.

"Yes," said Lidda. "Just. It didn't take much time to get out after we reversed the gate. No monsters to slow us down, just fields on fields of slush. Crops are destroyed, fields in ruin, and the bulk of the ice remains. It will melt, but the region's going to be a mess for a few years."

"Sonja?" Hennet didn't need to ask what happened to her. He knew.

"She's still alive," Lidda reminded him. "If any human is equipped to survive on the Plane of Ice, that's Sonja. And I bet she'll do everything she can to return."

Despite Lidda's comforting words, Hennet's eyes showed little hope.

"If you feel strong enough," Lidda said, "I can get you something to eat or drink. Regdar's down in the bar. Everybody in the city wants to buy us an ale and hear the stories of our exploits."

"I'm starving, Lidda. That would be terrific," said Hennet. He rubbed his cheek. The stinging sensation was gone. "And send Regdar up. I'd like to talk to him."

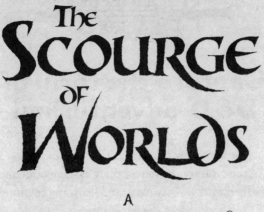

The SCOURGE OF WORLDS

A
DUNGEONS & DRAGONS®
Adventure

It's an interactive journey unlike any other - the quest to prevent the powerful "Scourge of Worlds" from falling into the wrong hands. Create a different adventure each time you watch.

An interactive moving coming to DVD Summer 2003.

COMING SOON:
www.scourgeofworlds.com for a preview.

Capture the thrill of D&D® adventuring!

These six new titles from T.H. Lain put you
in the midst of the heroic party as it encounters
deadly magic, sinister plots, and fearsome creatures.
Join the adventure!

THE BLOODY EYE
January 2003

TREACHERY'S WAKE
March 2003

PLAGUE OF ICE
May 2003

THE SUNDERED ARMS
July 2003

RETURN OF THE DAMNED
October 2003

THE DEATH RAY
December 2003

R.A. Salvatore's
War of the Spider Queen

Chaos has come to the Underdark
like never before.

New in hardcover!

CONDEMNATION, *Book III*
Richard Baker

The search for answers to Lolth's silence uncovers only more complex
questions. Doubt and frustration test the boundaries of already tenuous
relationships as members of the drow expedition begin to turn on each other.
Sensing the holes in the armor of Menzoberranzan, a new, dangerous threat
steps in to test the resolve of the Jewel of the Underdark, and finds it lacking.

May 2003

Now in paperback!

DISSOLUTION, *Book I*
Richard Lee Byers

When the Queen of the Demonweb Pits stops answering the prayers of her
faithful, the delicate balance of power that sustains drow civilization crumbles. As
the great Houses scramble for answers, Menzoberranzan herself begins to burn.

August 2003

INSURRECTION, *Book II*
Thomas M. Reid

The effects of Lolth's silence ripple through the Underdark and shake the drow
city of Ched Nasad to its very foundations. Trapped in a city on the edge of
oblivion, a small group of drow finds unlikely allies and a thousand new enemies.

October 2003

The foremost tales of the FORGOTTEN REALMS® series, brought together in these two great collections!

LEGACY OF THE DROW COLLECTOR'S EDITION
R.A. Salvatore

Here are the four books that solidified both the reputation of *New York Times* best-selling author R.A. Salvatore as a master of fantasy, and his greatest creation Drizzt as one of the genre's most beloved characters. Spanning the depths of the Underdark and the sweeping vistas of Icewind Dale, Legacy of the Drow is epic fantasy at its best.

January 2003

THE BEST OF THE REALMS
A FORGOTTEN REALMS anthology

Chosen from the pages of nine FORGOTTEN REALMS anthologies by readers like you, *The Best of the Realms* collects your favorite stories from the past decade. *New York Times* best-selling author R.A. Salvatore leads off the collection with an all-new story that will surely be among the best of the Realms!

November 2003

FORGOTTEN REALMS

Starlight & Shadows

New York Times best-selling author Elaine
Cunningham finally completes this stirring trilogy
of dark elf Liriel Baenre's travels across Faerûn!
All three titles feature stunning art from award-
winning fantasy artist Todd Lockwood.

New paperback editions!

DAUGHTER OF THE DROW
Book 1

Liriel Baenre, a free-spirited drow princess, ventures beyond the dark halls
of Menzoberranzan into the upper world. There, in the world of light, she
finds friendship, magic, and battles that will test her body and soul.

February 2003

TANGLED WEBS
Book 2

Liriel and Fyodor, her barbarian companion, walk the twisting streets of
Skullport in search of adventure. But the dark hands of Liriel's past still
reach out to clutch her and drag her back to the Underdark.

March 2003

New in hardcover – the long-awaited finale!

WINDWALKER
Book 3

Their quest complete, Liriel and Fyodor set out for the barbarian's homeland
to return the magical Windwalker amulet. Amid the witches of Rashemen,
Liriel learns of new magic and love and finds danger everywhere.

April 2003

The Minotaur Wars

From *New York Times* best-selling author Richard A. Knaak comes a powerful new chapter in the DRAGONLANCE® saga.

The continent of Ansalon, reeling from the destruction of the War of Souls, slowly crawls from beneath the rubble to rebuild – but the fires of war, once stirred, are difficult to quench. Another war comes to Ansalon, one that will change the balance of power throughout Krynn.

NIGHT OF BLOOD
Volume I

Change comes violently to the land of the minotaurs. Usurpers overthrow the emperor, murder all rivals, and dishonor minotaur tradition. The new emperor's wife presides over a cult of the dead, while the new government makes a secret pact with a deadly enemy. But betrayal is never easy, and rebellion lurks in the shadows.

The Minotaur Wars begin June 2003.

The original Chronicles

From *New York Times* best-selling authors Margaret Weis & Tracy Hickman

These classics of modern fantasy literature – the three titles that started it all – are available for the very first time in individual hardcover volumes. All three titles feature stunning cover art from award-winning artist Matt Stawicki.

DRAGONS OF AUTUMN TWILIGHT
Volume I
Friends meet amid a growing shadow of fear and rumors of war.
Out of their story, an epic saga is born.

January 2003

DRAGONS OF WINTER NIGHT
Volume II
Dragons return to Krynn as the Queen of Darkness launches her assault.
Against her stands a small band of heroes bearing a new weapon:
the DRAGONLANCE.

July 2003

DRAGONS OF SPRING DAWNING
Volume III
As the War of the Lance reaches its height, old friends clash amid
gallantry and betrayal. Yet their greatest battles lie within each of them.

November 2003

Legend of the
Five Rings

The Four Winds Saga

Only one can claim the Throne of Rokugan.

WIND OF JUSTICE
Third Scroll
Rich Wulf

Naseru, the most cold-hearted and scheming of the royal heirs, will
stop at nothing to sit upon the Throne of Rokugan. But when dark
forces in the City of Night threaten his beloved Empire, Naseru
must learn to wield the most unlikely weapon of all — justice.

June 2003

WIND OF TRUTH
Fourth Scroll
Ree Soesbee

Sezaru, one of the most powerful wielders of magic in all Rokugan,
has never desired his father's throne, but destiny calls to the son
of Toturi. Here, in the final volume of the Four Winds Saga,
all will be decided.

December 2003

Now available:

THE STEEL THRONE
Prelude
Edward Bolme

WIND OF HONOR
First Scroll
Ree Soesbee

WIND OF WAR
Second Scroll
Jess Lebow